Time seemed to stand still. The house was unusually quiet, with only the ticking of the kitchen clock on the wall beside them to tell of the passing of time.

Molly's mouth had gone dry, and colour warmed her cheeks as she saw Gideon's dark gaze follow the movement of her tongue across her lips.

She could barely breathe, was aware of Gideon with every sense and nerve of her body— aware of him in a way she had never been aware of any man before.

What would he say, this man who believed she had been his brother James's mistress, if the two of them were ever to make love and he discovered that she had never had a lover— that, at twenty-nine, she was still a virgin?

D1099685

Carole Mortimer was born in England, the youngest of three children. She began writing in 1978, and has now written over ninety books for Harlequin Mills and Boon®. Carole has four sons, Matthew, Joshua, Timothy and Peter, and a bearded collie called Merlyn. She says, 'I'm happily married to Peter senior; we're best friends as well as lovers, which is probably the best recipe for a successful relationship. We live on the Isle of Man.'

Recent titles by the same author:

HIS BID FOR A BRIDE
THE DESERVING MISTRESS
THE UNWILLING MISTRESS
HIS CINDERELLA MISTRESS

CLAIMING HIS CHRISTMAS BRIDE

BY
CAROLE MORTIMER

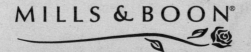

MILLS & BOON®

First published in Great Britain 2004
Harlequin Mills & Boon Limited,
Eton House, 18-24 Paradise Road, Richmond, Surrey TW9 1SR

© Carole Mortimer 2004

ISBN 0 263 83794 7

Set in Times Roman 10½ on 12 pt.
01-1204-45647

Printed and bound in Spain
by Litografia Rosés, S.A., Barcelona

CHAPTER ONE

'I REALIZE this is a christening, but isn't it a little early in the day's proceedings to be wetting the baby's head?'

Caught in the act of raising the glass of champagne to her lips, Molly froze. Unfortunately, the bubbly wine in the glass didn't freeze, too, slopping over the side to splash over her hand and down her wrist, instantly soaking into the sleeve of her jacket.

'Even for you,' that taunting voice added derisively.

Molly looked up indignantly, glaring across at the man who stood in the doorway watching her with hooded eyes so dark a blue they were almost the same colour as the iris.

Gideon Webber...!

She closed her eyes briefly. It had to be *him* who caught her guzzling a glass of champagne, didn't it? It just had to be!

He was the reason she had sneaked in here for this illicit glass of champagne in the first place, knowing she was going to need every bit of help she could find to face him later on this morning.

Except it wasn't later. It was now. And as she glanced back across at Gideon Webber she could see that same look of contempt on his arrogant face as had been there the last time she had seen him. The first as well as the last!

Not that the man looked any less lethally attractive than he had just over three years ago, when they had last met; his hair was that strange but attractive mixture of golden blond and molasses, his eyes that deep cobalt-blue, his nose long and arrogant, over a finely chiselled mouth, his chin square and determined. The last time Molly had seen him he had been wearing casual denims and a tee shirt, but today he looked even more arrogantly attractive in the formal dark suit and snowy white shirt, the latter complementing his golden tan.

Which he had no doubt recently acquired at some expensive ski resort—it was all right for some! Molly thought uncharitably.

'And what's that supposed to mean?' she snapped, even as she put the glass down on the table. She reached into her bag to look for the tissue she had put in there earlier for emergencies, having decided she had to be ready for any eventuality today! The last thing she wanted was to start sniffing in the middle of her nephew's christening.

Gideon Webber shrugged broad shoulders, the slightly contemptuous smile still curving that arrogant mouth. 'You seem to be rather—fond of—the odd glass or six, shall we say?' He arched mocking brows.

'No, we will not say!' Molly returned waspishly, stuffing the ineffectual tissue back in her bag. The sleeve of her jacket was still soaking wet. She just hoped it wouldn't stain when it dried; she had paid a lot of money for the new suit she was wearing in honour of the day.

Gideon Webber grimaced unrepentantly. 'We've only met twice—and both times you've had a glass in your hand!'

'The last time it was Alka-Seltzer,' she defended with another resentful glare.

'So it was,' he acknowledged with hard mockery. 'I remember commenting at the time that you would probably have been better downing another glass of whatever had put you in that state in the first place!'

Molly drew in a sharp breath as he made no effort to hide his deliberately insulting tone.

She had been dreading today anyway, ever since Crystal had told her who Peter's two godfathers were to be. But she had finally convinced herself that surely Gideon Webber was too polite to make any reference to their last memorable meeting. Obviously, in light of their present conversation, it was a totally erroneous assumption for her to have made about this—this—

This what? she questioned herself heavily.

Under any other circumstances she would have considered this man lethally attractive, 'drop-dead gorgeous', as some of her more colourful friends might have said. And he *was* gorgeous, no doubt about that— over six feet of lethal attraction. He just also happened to be one of the few people who had ever seen her the worse for wear because of too much alcohol...!

Time to take a bit more control of this conversation, she decided firmly. 'Those were exceptional circumstances,' she told him decisively.

He raised blond brows over enigmatic blue eyes. 'And today?'

'Oh, for goodness' sake,' Molly snapped impatiently. 'At most, I've had two sips of champagne.' She picked up the glass to take another assertive swallow. 'That makes three now.' She looked across at him challengingly.

He gave an acknowledging inclination of his head. 'If you say so,' he drawled.

Molly felt the colour enter her cheeks at this obvious scepticism as to the amount of champagne she had actually imbibed—a colour that didn't exactly go with her blaze of rich Titian hair. But, damn it, the man was making it sound as if she were some sort of alcoholic who sneaked around swigging alcohol whenever there was no one else around—

Wasn't that exactly what she had just been doing?

Well…yes. But—

She gave an irritable sigh. 'I do say so.' She nodded curtly. 'I was just—it was only—' Oh, give up, Molly, she advised herself self-disgustedly— While you're not ahead! 'Shouldn't we all be leaving for the church?' she prompted briskly.

'Crys sent me in search of you for just that reason,' Gideon Webber confirmed dryly.

Crys had sent this man to find her? But why not? Crys, of all people, could have no idea how much Molly had dreaded seeing him again. And that was the way she wanted it to stay!

She put the champagne glass down on the table. 'I'm ready if you are.'

He gave a mocking inclination of his head before turning to open the door for her. 'After you,' he invited smoothly.

Molly straightened her shoulders, aware of that hooded gaze following every inch of her progress, knowing what he would see, too: a small redhead with warm brown eyes—eyes usually full of fun and laughter!—dressed formally today, in a dress and matching jacket, her legs shapely, the heels on her shoes a little high for comfort, but their colour exactly matching that of her suit.

'Just one more thing,' Gideon Webber murmured softly as she would have passed him in the doorway.

She raised wary eyes, suddenly tense. 'Yes…?' she prompted cautiously, wondering what the 'one more thing' he wanted to say to her could possibly be. Apart from mentioning their unforgettable first meeting, of course!

He gave a humourless smile, that gleam of white teeth looking almost feral. 'Has anyone ever mentioned to you that women with red hair shouldn't wear certain shades of pink?'

His remark was so unexpected, so insulting in view of the fact that she did have red hair, and that the suit she was wearing was pink, that for several seconds all Molly could do was open and shut her mouth like a goldfish in a bowl, with no actual sound passing her lips.

She had loved the style of the dress and jacket as soon as she'd seen them in the shop, but although she often did wear pink, had been a little unsure about this particular pale shade, debating long and hard while in the shop and trying the suit on whether or not it was actually the right colour for her. The shop assistant, probably sensing her uncertainty, and, in retrospect, probably feeling in danger of losing her commission on a sale, had assured Molly that she looked wonderful in it.

So much for wonderful!

Her eyes sparkled angrily as she turned to give Gideon Webber a haughty glare. 'Most men would be too polite to say such a thing,' she bit out scathingly.

Humour glinted in his eyes now. 'Most men couldn't tell you what any woman was wearing yesterday—let alone whether or not it suited her!'

He had a point there, Molly acknowledged ruefully, thinking affectionately of her stepfather. As long as her mother wasn't actually walking around in something indecent, she was sure Matthew wouldn't notice what Caroline was actually wearing.

'I—'

'Molly!' Crys cried thankfully as she spotted them at the end of the hallway. 'And Gideon,' she added with even more relief, strolling down the hallway to link her arm with Molly's. 'We thought the two of you must have decided you didn't want to be Peter's godparents after all and run away together!'

Molly gave a disbelieving snort at this possible scenario, not even daring to look at Gideon Webber for his own reaction to the remark. She was easily able to guess at the derision that would be curling those arrogant lips.

Especially as she was wearing a shade of pink that clashed with her red hair!

Damn him for telling her that; she now felt decidedly uncomfortable in the suit, what little confidence the champagne had given her evaporating like mist.

But she still had the christening and the rest of the day to get through yet. After that she could scream and stamp her feet in the privacy of the guest bedroom on the third floor above them!

She and Crystal had been friends since schooldays, going their separate ways careerwise after that. Crys had become a first-class chef before opening and running a successful restaurant, as well as appearing in her own cookery programme, and Molly had chosen to go into acting.

Crys had also married three and a half years ago, that marriage tragically coming to an end when her husband, James, died of cancer only months later. But to Molly's delight Crys had met and married Molly's stepbrother Sam almost two years ago, and the couple now had three-month-old Peter James. Hence this christening, three days before Christmas.

The only fly in the ointment—in fact the only cloud on Molly's present horizon!—was that Sam and Crys had asked her previous brother-in-law, James's older brother Gideon, to be one of Peter's godfathers. An honour, Crys had informed Molly happily, he had been only too pleased to accept.

Which had put Molly in something of a quandary. She didn't have happy memories of her one and only meeting with Gideon Webber, and she was sure his own feelings towards her were somewhat less than cordial. But as she had already been asked by Sam and Crys to be Peter's godmother, and had readily accepted, she could hardly turn round and tell them she had changed her mind because Gideon Webber was one of the godfathers, now, could she?

Of course she couldn't, and so she had armed herself with every feminine weapon she could think of to give her the self-confidence she needed to face the man: new hairstyle, professional make-up, new clothes and shoes. Even a surreptitious glass of champagne to give her an extra boost! She just hadn't taken into account the fact that Gideon Webber, like his younger brother, was an interior designer. And that he would instinctively know she was wearing a shade of pink that didn't go with her red hair!

But at least Crys had interrupted the exchange, and spared her any further insults from the man.

In the rush that followed their mass departure, Molly found herself in a car with her stepfather on the way to the church in this ruggedly beautiful part of Yorkshire where Crys and Sam lived most of the time now. Her mother and the second godfather had elected to travel with Gideon Webber in his dark green Jaguar, and Sam and Crys were travelling separately with Peter James.

Merlin, Sam's Irish Wolfhound and Peter James's guardian from the very first day the baby had arrived home from the hospital where he had been born, sat forlornly on the driveway, watching their departure with the obvious intention of waiting there until they returned with his precious charge.

'Matthew, what is Mum wearing today?' Molly prompted casually.

'Wearing?' Matthew repeated frowningly as he concentrated on following Sam's car the short distance to the church.

'Yes—wearing,' Molly confirmed dryly. 'As in colour?' she added helpfully.

Her stepfather's frown deepened as he obviously gave the question some thought. 'Well,' he finally said consideringly, 'it's a sort of blue thing. Or possibly green. A dress, I think. Or it might be a jacket and skirt. In any case, I'm almost certain it's blue or green,' he added, with a decisive nod of his head.

Molly had already seen her mother on her arrival a little over an hour ago, and knew for a fact that the 'blue or green' suit, of whatever description, was actually a dress and long jacket in a beautiful shade of turquoise. Which, to most men, probably could be described as 'blue or green'…!

And that, in Molly's estimation, just went to prove that Gideon Webber wasn't like other men!

Well, she already knew that, Molly acknowledged with a sigh as she turned to look out of the car window at the Yorkshire Moors.

How she wished today were already over. Then she could get on with enjoying Christmas with Crys, Sam and baby Peter James. Her parents were leaving tomorrow on an extended cruise to somewhere warmer than England—which was probably just about anywhere in December—and so wouldn't be here for the holidays, which was why they were having the christening today, before the parents' departure for warmer climes.

After all, what was it? Molly reasoned with herself. One day. Not even that, really. Just a few hours. And then Gideon Webber would depart and the four of them could get on with anticipating Christmas.

But those next few hours, spent in Gideon Webber's acerbic company, could feel like a lifetime if he continued with the insults!

'Glass of champagne?'

Molly turned frowningly towards the sound of that voice, her frown dissipating as she recognised David Strong, an actor who starred in a television series written by her stepbrother, Sam. David was Peter's other godfather.

Tall, dark and ruggedly handsome, aged in his early forties, David brought his own brand of charm to the television series *Bailey*. But he had been widowed several months ago, when his wife had been killed in a car accident, and the sadness in his eyes and the lines beside his mouth, despite the warmth of his smile, were testament to his recent grief.

'Thanks.' Molly accepted the glass he held out to her. Having met David socially several times before, she was perfectly relaxed in his company.

Though she couldn't repress her furtive glance around the room to check whether or not Gideon Webber was watching her accept the glass of champagne, and she frowned her irritation as he raised his own glass of what appeared to be sparkling water to her across Crys and Sam's crowded sitting-room.

Molly turned quickly away from the easily discernible mocking humour in those dark blue eyes, the unbecoming colour once again flooding her freckle-covered cheeks. Damn the man. What was he? A one-man vigilante on the consumption of alcohol? Or was it just her consumption…?

Probably, she accepted heavily, wishing once again it had been anyone else but him who had seen her condition on that morning just over three years ago.

Although the world of acting was very often awash with the stuff, Molly very rarely drank alcohol herself—had found that it didn't mix with early set calls or late-night theatre appearances. Which was probably why the downing of that bottle of wine just over three years ago had completely knocked her off her feet!

But there had been good reason for that, she reminded herself defensively. Knowing yourself in love with a married man—a married man who assured you he had every intention of remaining that way—would induce any sane woman to turn to the bottle. Besides, it had only been one measly bottle of white wine—not the whole crateful Gideon Webber seemed to be implying!

Did wine come in a crate? she wondered illogically, or—?

Get a grip, Barton, she instructed herself severely, determinedly turning her attention to David Strong. After all, he was almost as good-looking as Gideon Webber—and much nicer to boot!

'It's good to see you again, David,' she told him warmly.

'And you.' He nodded, brown eyes crinkling at the

corners as he smiled. 'Although from what I hear we should be seeing a lot more of each other in the near future...?' He raised dark brows questioningly.

Ah. Obviously someone had told him. Possibly Sam, as a courtesy to the leading man in his award-winning television series? Or had the secret leaked out in some other way? Probably the latter, she accepted ruefully; the supposed secrecy of the acting world had more holes in it than a sieve!

She gave David a quizzical smile. 'Do you mind?'

'Not at all,' he answered easily, giving her the famous grin that had made him such a hit with female television viewers. 'I think it's past time Bailey had a more permanent love-interest in his life,' he added reassuringly.

That wasn't quite what Molly had meant by her question. It was one thing having the writer of a television series pop up in the studio whenever he felt like it—as Sam often did—it was quite another to have that writer's stepsister appearing in the series with you. As the main character's permanent but definitely whacky girlfriend!

Molly had been working mainly in American theatre the last few years, with the occasional television role thrown in, and until recently had had every intention of remaining out there. But a couple of months ago Sam had sent her the first script he had written for the new *Bailey* series, due to begin filming in the New Year, along with a cryptic message. 'As I wrote the Daisy role based on you, only you could possible play her! Come home. I need you.' Enough to evoke anyone's curiosity.

Although Molly hadn't been quite so sure after reading the script of that one episode!

The character of Daisy was an outgoing, dangerously inquisitive private detective, endearingly naive when it came to the vagaries of human nature, and most of all accident-prone—to the point where objects—usually bodies—seemed literally to throw themselves in her path for her to fall over.

Based on her? she had wondered, slightly dazed. She was outgoing, yes, and could be slightly eccentric, yes. But she wasn't too sure that any of the other character traits fitted her, no matter what Sam might think to the contrary...

But the director of the programme had seemed happy enough with her audition when she'd returned to England a couple of weeks ago, and hadn't hesitated about offering her a contract to cover the next *Bailey* series.

She had thought that particular snippet of information hadn't yet been leaked, but obviously she was wrong; it was one of those well-guarded secrets that everyone knew about!

'I actually meant, do you mind that I'm going to appear in the *Bailey* series with you?' Molly corrected ruefully.

David raised dark brows. 'The director assures me you were brilliant at your audition; why should I mind?'

She gave an awkward shrug. 'Well...Sam is my brother.' She pointed out the obvious. 'And I wouldn't like you to think—some people might think that had something to do with my getting the part.' She grimaced.

'The word you're looking for is nepotism,' drawled an insulting voice.

Gideon Webber's voice. Of course. He seemed to lose no opportunity to insult her.

Was it acceptable for the godmother to hit one of the godfathers at a christening party? Molly wondered angrily.

Probably not.

Pity.

'Gideon!' David greeted the other man warmly—giving Molly the necessary time to clasp her hands tightly together in order not to give in to her initial impulse, after all. 'It's really good to see you again,' the actor added smilingly.

Again? Molly wondered frowningly. Since when did television actors' and interior designers' paths ever cross? Never, or so she had hoped when she had decided on this move back to England. Although it now appeared she might have been wrong about that...

'You can forget nepotism,' David added with a grin. 'From all accounts, this little lady can act her socks off.'

'And any other part of her clothing. Or so I'm led to believe,' Gideon Webber returned dryly.

Molly's gasp of indignation was lost in David's roar of laughter. Obviously he thought the other man was just joking. Molly knew better.

She looked up at Gideon Webber with narrowed eyes. His expression was openly scathing, and the colour slowly crept up into her cheeks. Exactly what had he meant by that remark?

'How did you know she has to take her clothes off in episode four?' David prompted the other man humorously.

Gideon's gaze didn't waver from Molly's as he answered the other man. 'Just an educated guess.'

Molly had no privacy to digest what David had just said. She had to take her clothes off?

Having only returned from America a couple of

weeks ago, and been busy since then moving into the flat she had found in London, there hadn't been time yet for her to read any of the other episodes in the new *Bailey* series.

She didn't have a bad figure, definitely had curves in all the right places, but nevertheless Molly wasn't sure she wanted to take all her clothes off for public display. Even with someone as nice as David.

And, if the derisive look on Gideon Webber's face was anything to go by, he didn't think her body was good enough for public display, either...

CHAPTER TWO

DAMNED cheek!

There was nothing wrong with her body—no excess bulges, her breasts pert, her waist narrow, hips slender, legs shapely—so why didn't Gideon Webber think she was up to playing a nude scene?

Molly angled her chin challengingly at Gideon before turning to smile at David. 'I think it might be rather fun,' she assured him airily, hoping that none of her inner trepidation showed.

Until this moment there had been no mention of the fact that she had to appear nude in episode four or anywhere else. And she had signed the contract now!

Just wait until she got hold of Sam!

'So do I.' David grinned boyishly. 'I have to say that Sam's happy marriage to Crys has certainly livened the series up!'

So it would appear. She really did need to talk to Sam—if only to see if there were any other surprises that he hadn't told her about.

'They are happy together, aren't they?' Gideon murmured ruefully, looking across now to where Sam and Crys were talking softly together, their eyes glowing with the love they felt for each other, which had only deepened on the birth of their son.

'Of course they are,' Molly said waspishly, frowning.

Surely this man, just because Crys had once been married to his younger brother, didn't begrudge her the happiness she had now found with Sam?

Molly knew that Crys had loved James very much, but she was only twenty-nine now—the same age as Molly herself. Surely Gideon didn't think Crys should have remained faithful to his brother's memory for the rest of her life? If he did, then he should never have agreed to be Peter's godfather.

Gideon turned back to her, blue eyes hard as sapphires. 'Then let's hope they stay that way,' he bit out harshly.

Molly's frown deepened. 'Why shouldn't they?'

'I think those two have already had their fair share of bad luck where love is concerned.' David was the one to put this in quietly.

Molly knew exactly what bad luck David was referring to: Crys's past loss was obvious enough, and Sam hadn't looked at a woman until Crys after being publicly persecuted by his ex-fiancée twelve years before.

But, after David's own recent loss, it was insensitive of Molly and Gideon to be carrying out this conversation in front of him at all. Even if the antagonism between the two of them was so intense it could be cut with a knife.

'You're right, David,' Molly soothed, putting an apologetic hand on his arm. 'Isn't he, Gideon?' she prompted hardly.

'I think so—yes,' Gideon agreed lightly, but a much stronger emotion burned briefly in the darkness of his gaze as he continued to look down at Molly.

And just what did he mean by that remark? And that look?

This man was too deep for her, too enigmatic; in fact, she could definitely feel a headache coming on!

She drew in a sharp breath as she deliberately turned away from that compelling gaze. 'If you'll both excuse me...? I just want to go and spend a few minutes with my parents before they leave,' she added apologetically, knowing her parents had to go shortly.

'Don't let me stop you,' Gideon Webber assured her abruptly.

If he so wanted to avoid her company, then why had he come over here and joined in this conversation at all? Molly wondered bad-temperedly.

'See you later.' David had recovered enough from the reminder of his recent loss to smile at her.

'Of course,' Molly said gently, not even sparing Gideon Webber a second glance before walking away to join her parents as they stood together across the room.

Damn the man. Damn. Damn. Damn!

Today's christening should have been a wonderful family occasion, full of warmth and love, with all of them doting on Peter James. Instead, because of Gideon Webber's presence, it had become something of a nightmare for Molly. But it was a nightmare she intended putting an end to at the earliest opportunity.

'You!' Molly gasped her dismay the following morning as she entered the kitchen to get herself a cup of coffee and found herself confronted by Gideon Webber, obviously doing exactly the same thing.

She had managed to excuse herself from the christening party the day before as soon as her parents had left, her claim of a headache completely genuine by that time.

She had certainly had no idea that Gideon Webber had spent the night here, too.

'Me,' he confirmed, his smile taunting her obvious

displeasure at finding him here. 'Coffee?' He held up the coffee-pot in his hand.

A brandy would have been preferable after the shock she had just received. But that would only confirm for this man that she was some sort of dipsomaniac!

'Thank you,' Molly managed to squeak, through a throat that suddenly seemed extremely dry and lips that had gone numb.

What was he still doing here? she wondered wildly.

Unusually for December, the sun was actually shining, and the birds had been singing, too, as Molly made her way lightly down the stairs, filling her with pleasurable anticipation for the day ahead.

Anticipation that had just taken a definite nosedive!

'Here—drink some of this.' Gideon pushed a mug of steaming coffee into her unresisting hand. 'Headache still bad?' he prompted mockingly.

He was the headache! And, yes, it was bad—a terrible pounding had started behind her eyes and it hadn't been there seconds ago.

'I wasn't sure whether or not you took sugar,' he drawled as she sat down to take a much-needed swallow of the coffee—and almost choked on it. Not only was it unsweetened, it was also strong enough to strip the enamel from her teeth.

'It's fine,' she managed to gasp, her eyes watering from the resounding slap Gideon had given her on her back. The thin green jumper she wore with denims was no barrier against the force of that hand.

Why hadn't he just asked her how she liked her coffee? Or would that have been too easy?

Probably, Molly instantly answered herself irritably. It might also have deprived him of the pleasure of hitting her as well as choking her.

Okay, so he had stayed the night, for whatever reason. She accepted that, but that didn't answer the question: what was he still doing here?

'Crys and Sam have taken the baby and Merlin for a walk on the moors,' he supplied economically, before sitting down in the chair opposite hers across the kitchen table.

As she had been rather late coming down it didn't in the least surprise her that her stepbrother and Crys had already gone out for their usual morning walk with the dog. What she did find unsettling was the fact that she was left alone here for some time with a man who obviously despised her.

'Don't let me keep you from anything,' she invited stiffly as Gideon still sat across from her, calmly drinking his own strong coffee.

He raised mocking brows. 'What did you have in mind?'

She shrugged. 'Having your breakfast? Packing?' Leaving!

The sooner he made his departure, the sooner she could get on with relaxing—something she certainly couldn't do around this man, either physically or mentally. Every remark he made to her, it seemed, had some sort of double meaning.

'I don't fancy breakfast,' he answered her evenly. 'But you go ahead.'

'I'll pass, thanks.' She didn't fancy breakfast, either.

But what about his packing? He was dressed casually today, in fitted black denims and a deep blue tee shirt, which meant he had his suit from yesterday to pack, at least...

'It was a pity you left the party so early yesterday evening,' Gideon drawled lightly.

Surely he hadn't missed having her there? Or was it just that he hadn't had anyone to sharpen his rapier tongue on once she had gone upstairs to bed? That was probably nearer the truth.

'David had us all in hysterics with some of his more risqué stories of the acting profession,' Gideon enlightened her dryly.

She would just bet that he had. In her experience, there was always more action going on behind the scenes than in front of the camera. Although, thankfully, she had never worked with David before, so none of those stories could have been about her.

She gave a grimace of a smile. 'I'm sure we all have some of those we could relate.'

'Even you?'

Why had that sounded like *especially* you? Or was she just ultra-sensitive where this man was concerned? In the circumstances, was that so surprising?

She moistened dry lips. The strong coffee might have woken her up, but it had done very little to quench her morning thirst. 'Gideon, I think the two of us need to talk—'

'Morning, you two,' David greeted them heartily as he breezed into the kitchen, also dressed casually in denims and a tee shirt, his feet bare of socks and shoes, his dark hair still ruffled from sleep.

Molly stared up at him in stunned surprise; had David spent the night here, too? Obviously. It seemed she had missed more than risqué stories by going to bed early the evening before.

'I don't know whether it's the bracing Yorkshire air or the champagne I drank yesterday,' David said lightly as he moved to pour himself a mug of coffee, sipping at the strong brew with obvious enjoyment, 'but I slept better last night than I have for months,' he went on with satisfaction as he sat down at the table to join them. 'So, where's our godson this morning?' he prompted interestedly.

Their godson... For the first time Molly realised that the three of them were forever linked by this connection to Peter James. That wasn't so bad when it came to David, but Gideon Webber was another prospect altogether!

'Out for a walk with his parents and Merlin.' Gideon was the one to answer the other man. 'You'll have to excuse Molly, David; I don't think she's a morning person,' he told the other man dryly, before turning to look at her mockingly.

She wasn't at her best this morning, no, having so far received one surprise after another, but ordinarily she woke bright and ready for the new day.

Although somehow she didn't think Gideon was necessarily referring to *this* morning...

Her gaze narrowed as she glared at him. 'I'm not used to company in the morning,' she bit out tersely.

'Really?' He raised sceptical brows.

He *did* mean something else.

This man had judged and sentenced her on the evidence of that one morning just over three years ago—just one morning, when... When what?

When she had been tousle-haired and heavy-eyed from lack of sleep. When she had obviously been suffering from the effect of too much wine. When he had seen her dressed only in another man's shirt...

Yes, but...

Yes, but what? There was an explanation for all that Gideon had seen—or thought he had seen—but she very much doubted that this man wanted to hear it. Or whether he would believe it!

She stood up abruptly. 'I think I'll go for a walk outside and wait for Crys and Sam to come back,' she said tautly.

And she would hope that Gideon might have taken his leave before she came back. Although somehow she doubted he would leave without saying goodbye to Crys and Sam.

'If you hang on a minute while I put on some shoes I'll join you,' David told her as he stood up. 'Gideon?' he prompted brightly.

'You two go ahead.' He shook his head. 'I have a couple of calls I need to make this morning.'

'See you later, then.' David nodded, confirming that he, at least, expected to see more of Gideon today.

Which was no consolation to Molly at all as she waited outside for David to join her. If he was now making calls, exactly how long did Gideon Webber intend remaining here?

'What is it between you two?' David prompted a few minutes later as the two of them strolled across the gravel driveway. 'You and Gideon?' he enlightened her as she looked puzzled.

'Me and...? Nothing,' she scoffed forcefully. 'Absolutely nothing,' she repeated firmly as David didn't look convinced.

David quirked teasing brows. 'That wasn't the impression I got either yesterday or today. Come on, Molly, the two of us are going to be working together for months. I'm sure to find out if you're involved with anyone.' He grinned boyishly.

'Well, it certainly isn't Gideon Webber!' she snapped, two bright spots of angry colour in her cheeks now. 'The man does nothing but insult me every time he opens his mouth,' she added disgustedly, knowing it was the truth, and also well aware of the reason for it.

But what could she do about it? If she protested her innocence too strongly Gideon Webber was the sort of man who would only see her vehemence as an admission of guilt on her part. But not to protest was just as unacceptable—and more damning. It seemed that with this particular man she couldn't win.

Not that she hadn't had her share of romantic entanglements in the past, because she had. Gideon Webber just happened to have been a witness to the one time she had made a complete idiot of herself.

David chuckled. 'If we were all teenagers that would be a sure sign that Gideon likes you.'

'Well, we aren't,' Molly said disgruntledly. From the evidence she had seen so far Gideon Webber had never been a teenager—had just gone straight from babyhood to the acerbic man he now was. 'And I can assure you he doesn't.' She sighed heavily, knowing that Gideon's feelings towards her were much more complicated than that.

'More's the pity, hmm?' David teased.

'No, thanks.' Molly grimaced. 'The strong, silent type has never appealed to me,' she added derisively.

Although she had a definite feeling that as far as she was concerned Gideon wasn't going to remain 'silent' for long. At the moment his antagonism towards her was just bubbling below the surface, giving her the distinct feeling that it wouldn't stay that way for much longer, that he was going to have his say concerning their first meeting.

'If you say so,' David accepted teasingly, giving the

clear impression that he didn't believe her lack of interest in Gideon was genuine.

Well, David certainly wasn't in the minority when it came to that; Gideon obviously didn't believe a word she said, either.

'This is a great spot, isn't it?' David enthused happily as they strolled around the extensive grounds. 'I thought Sam was insane when he first decided to bury himself up here, but I can see the attraction now. Even more so now that he's married to Crys. You and she have been friends a long time, haven't you?' he prompted interestedly.

'Since school,' Molly confirmed.

'So you must have known James Webber, too.' David nodded.

Molly frowned at this mention of Gideon's younger brother, Crys's first husband. Her gaze narrowed and she looked sideways at David in search of any hidden meaning in his words. But he was totally engrossed in the rugged beauty that surrounded Falcon House, and was apparently just making conversation as they walked.

'Yes, I met James at university,' she said evenly. 'In fact, I introduced him to Crys,' she added wistfully. The guilt she felt at having ultimately caused Crys such unhappiness when James had died only months into their marriage had never been completely erased, despite Crys's now happy marriage to Sam.

David turned to her with raised brows. 'So you must have known Gideon, too? After all, the two brothers worked together.'

Thankfully, Gideon Webber, ten years older than his younger brother, had never been included in their group of friends. In fact, Molly had only met him the once. But that once had been quite enough, thank you!

She gave David a reproachful grimace. 'You really are wasting your time fishing in that particular direction, David—Gideon Webber and I dislike each other intensely.'

He made a face. 'Does Crys know that?'

She frowned. 'Of course not,' she dismissed abruptly. 'Why should she?'

David shrugged. 'Oh, it's only that... Ah, here they all are.' He nodded in the direction of the battered Land Rover coming up the driveway. 'Excuse me, won't you?' he added hastily as he turned back towards the house. 'But I don't think Merlin has made his mind up yet as to whether I'm friend or foe!'

Molly chuckled appreciatively as David beat a hasty retreat to the house; Merlin could appear quite intimidating until you got to know him. Or, more precisely, until he got to know you.

Having known the dog from when he was a puppy, Molly felt no such hesitation in waiting for her step-brother and Crys to get out of the car. Baby Peter was lifted from the back of the vehicle by his father, and Merlin followed quickly behind him.

'I thought I saw David with you.' Crys looked around frowningly after taking her son into her arms. She was ethereally lovely, with her silver-blond hair loose down her back, and the beauty of her face dominated by misty grey eyes. She was boyishly slender, in spite of having given birth to Peter James only months ago.

'You did.' Molly nodded, grinning. 'He seems to think Merlin needs a little more time to get used to him.'

Sam gave a rueful shake of his head as he absently stroked the huge dog behind the ears. 'I've assured him that Merlin won't bite him as long as he doesn't bite Merlin!'

'I'm sure that helped to convince him of Merlin's tameness.' Crys chuckled huskily. 'Time for breakfast, I think,' she announced briskly, placing the sleeping baby in Molly's arms. 'Pancakes all round!' she decided brightly as she walked towards the house.

Molly followed slowly behind Crys and Sam. Ordinarily she would have been one of the first to appreciate Crys's pancakes—they were to die for, light and fluffy, delicious with maple syrup or sugar. But not today. Not when the dark green Jaguar parked in the front driveway clearly told of Gideon Webber's presence inside the house still.

'Perhaps he'll choke on one of Mummy's pancakes,' Molly suggested hopefully to baby Peter as he opened his lids to look up at her with alert blue eyes. 'I know, I know, he's your godfather,' she accepted apologetically. 'But you do have another one—and I can hope, can't I?'

'Talking to yourself?' drawled a mockingly recognisable voice.

Molly looked up sharply to find Gideon Webber approaching the kitchen door from the front of the house, having moved so quietly she hadn't heard his footsteps on the gravel. Merlin obviously had, and was walking at the man's side, the two of them obviously happy in each other's company.

He raised dark brows derisively, obviously aware of her surprise at seeing him there. 'I had to get something from my car.'

Perhaps it was too much to hope that he had been putting his suitcase in the boot at the same time.

'I was talking to baby Peter, not myself,' she told him stiffly.

Gideon gave a mocking smile. 'Well, I suppose talking to a three-month-old baby has its pluses; at least he can't answer you back!'

Unlike this man, who seemed to have an answer to everything!

Molly eyed him scathingly. 'Unusual in a man,' she acknowledged dryly.

'In my experience, even more unusual in a woman,' Gideon murmured softly, before opening the door for her to enter the kitchen ahead of him, effectively cutting off any sharp retort she might have liked to make at this arrogantly sexist remark. And there were several she would have liked to make.

But the laughter and warmth in the kitchen, with Crys busy mixing pancakes, Sam and David helping to lay the table, the three of them talking as they worked, made her desire to snap a reply seem churlish.

Falcon House was a large, three-storey-high building, but Crys and Sam both loved their privacy, and they preferred to do most things in the house themselves. A woman came in from the village three afternoons a week to take care of any heavy housework that might need doing, but Crys did all the cooking herself.

Despite its obvious size, it was definitely a family home, full of warmth, love, and laughter, and Molly usually enjoyed her visits here enormously. Usually...

Why did Gideon Webber have to be here to ruin it all?

Although she had a feeling she was in the minority in feeling that way. David and Sam were obviously enjoying the other man's company, and Crys and Gideon were standing close together as he helped in the cooking of the pancakes, the two of them moving with an easy familiarity that spoke of a long friendship.

But was it just friendship, or did it go deeper than that? Molly wondered as she sat slightly apart from everyone else, still holding baby Peter as she silently watched them all. Certainly there was nothing more than that on Crys's side—Crys's love for Sam was absolute—but Gideon was definitely more at ease with Crys than Molly had seen him with anyone else. The two of them were talking softly together, Gideon smiling openly, his gaze warm as it rested on Crys—

Now what was she imagining? That perhaps Gideon was secretly in love with Crys? A man she had previously believed wasn't capable of feeling love for anyone?

Ridiculous, she admonished herself impatiently. Gideon had known Crys for years, he was her ex-brother-in-law—of course he had feelings for her; it was only Molly's own resentment towards the man that saw it as possibly being anything else.

'All right?' Sam prompted softly, having come to stand beside her without Molly even being aware of it.

She pushed her troubling thoughts firmly to the back of her mind, looking up to smile at her stepbrother. As well as being a highly successful screenwriter, Sam was the epitome of tall, dark and handsome, and Molly had adored him from the moment she'd known her mother was to marry his father seventeen years ago.

'Of course,' she assured him brightly. 'How could I not be when I'm holding my favourite nephew?' she added teasingly.

Sam came down on his haunches beside her, briefly touching his son's cheek in wonder. 'Your only nephew—unless you know something I don't?' He looked lovingly across the room to where Crys was laughingly serving pancakes.

'Not at all,' Molly chucklingly assured him as he turned back to her.

'Does it make you feel in the least broody yourself?' Sam asked shrewdly.

That was a little harder to answer. She wasn't even involved with anyone at the moment, had severed what had only been a casual relationship with a fellow actor before leaving New York. But she was twenty-nine now, the same age as Crys, and, if she were honest with herself, she envied her friend her loving husband and beautiful baby.

For all the good that would do her, Molly reproved herself ruefully. Without a man in her life, loving or otherwise, there would be no family of her own, either.

She grimaced. 'Sam, I doubt it's escaped your notice that I'm not involved with anyone just now.'

He shrugged. 'What do you think of David and Gideon?'

Molly frowned her puzzlement at this abrupt turn in the conversation. 'What do I think of them as what?'

It was Sam's turn to grimace. 'Well, I think Crys has one of them in mind as your future husband and father of your children.'

'She *what*?' Molly gasped her bewilderment, sitting rigidly in her chair now, unable to hide her horror at what Sam was suggesting.

'Don't tell her I said anything,' Sam told her hastily. 'I think it's all this domesticity that's gone to her head and infused her with this desire to matchmake for you,' he added affectionately. 'She wants everyone to be as happy as we are.'

Molly blinked dazedly. 'Yes, but—'

'Crys assures me that David and Gideon are both extremely eligible men,' her stepbrother teased.

'They may be—' her voice rose slightly '—but David was only recently widowed. And as for Gideon—I don't happen to—'

'Not a word to Crys about any of this, Molly,' Sam warned softly as plates were put on the table. 'She won't be very happy with me if she knows I've said anything to you.'

'But—'

'I'll put Peter in his cradle and then we can all have breakfast.' He spoke normally as he bent to take Peter and crossed the room to put him in the cradle that stood in the corner of the kitchen.

Molly stared after him, totally bewildered by their conversation.

What did he mean, Crys was matchmaking between her and David or Gideon? She wasn't due to start working with David until the end of January, and after today she hoped never to meet Gideon Webber ever again, so exactly when was this matchmaking supposed to take place?

She had a definite feeling she wasn't going to like the answer to that question.

CHAPTER THREE

'EVERYONE had enough to eat?' Crys prompted happily half an hour later.

Half an hour during which Molly's bewilderment hadn't lessened in the least. She knew that Crys was happier now than she had ever been, and that this second marriage to Sam was her whole life, but it certainly hadn't occurred to Molly that her best friend might decide it was high time that *she* found such happiness—to the point that she had already picked out two eligible men for her to look over as prospective husband material.

David Strong and Gideon Webber, of all people...

David was one of the nicest men Molly had ever met, and instantly put one at ease, but he was still suffering badly from the unexpected death of his wife. Molly was very much looking forward to working with him, but she knew he certainly wasn't on the look-out for another woman in his life in the near future.

As for Gideon Webber...!

The only consolation to her own aversion to such an idea was that, much as he obviously loved Crys, Molly knew Gideon Webber would be furious at the very idea of being matched with her.

'There's a good reason behind my wife's desire to make sure you're all well fed,' Sam remarked dryly after they had all assured Crys they couldn't eat another thing.

Crys grinned unrepentantly. 'With all the excitement

and preparation for the christening we haven't had time to put up our Christmas decorations yet,' she explained. 'Sam has some telephone calls to return in his study this morning and so I thought the four of us might have some fun putting up the decorations.'

'No problem,' David assured instantly.

'Glad to help,' Gideon added lightly.

Molly was so disturbed by this added delay to the two men leaving that she didn't say anything.

'You haven't heard where the decorations are yet,' Sam warned them wryly.

David chuckled, shaking his head as he looked at Crys. 'Your wife has the ability to charm the birds out of the trees, Sam,' he drawled affectionately.

'Or the decorations out of the attic?' Sam suggested ruefully.

'That, too,' Gideon acknowledged dryly as he joined in the teasing conversation.

It made Molly feel more out of things than ever; this Christmas holiday simply wasn't working out in the way that she had thought it would.

'How about you, Molly?' Sam turned to her as he, not unusually, seemed to sense some of her confusion. The two of them had always been closer than blood brother and sister. 'I was going to take Peter in with me this morning, but if you would rather look after him than help with the decorations...?'

She would rather do anything else other than spend the morning in Gideon Webber's company.

But even as she opened her mouth to accept Sam's let-out she found her gaze caught and held by Gideon's taunting one. Delicate colour rose in her cheeks and she knew he was aware, and obviously enjoying, her discomfort in his presence.

Her mouth set stubbornly and her eyes flashed before she turned to smile at Sam. 'Thanks for the offer, but you know how I've always loved putting up Christmas decorations.' And how little chance she had had to do so during her years in America.

It simply hadn't seemed worth the effort to put up Christmas decorations in her apartment these last few years, when there had been only herself to see them. She had been looking forward to being involved in all aspects of this family Christmas, including putting up the decorations, and she wasn't going to let Gideon Webber's presence ruin that for her.

'I certainly do.' Sam ruffled her hair affectionately. 'When she was younger she used to insist the decorations went up in November and didn't come down until February!' he confided in the others.

The colour deepened in Molly's cheeks, and she carefully avoided looking in Gideon's direction this time, sure those dark blue eyes would be filled with mockery. 'I'm not quite that bad any more.' She grimaced self-consciously. 'But I have always loved Christmas,' she admitted ruefully.

'Nothing wrong with that,' David assured her approvingly.

'Nothing at all,' Gideon agreed huskily.

Molly looked up at him sharply, expecting to see the normal derision in his gaze, but instead she found him looking at her quizzically, his thoughts unreadable. What now? she wondered frowningly.

Gideon gave a mocking inclination of his head. 'I've always thought that anyone who likes Christmas can't be all bad,' he drawled challengingly.

Brown eyes warred with dark blue for several long seconds before Molly broke the gaze to look at the other three people in the room; Crys still smiled warmly, David and Sam were busy clearing the table of the debris from breakfast.

Was she, Molly, the only one who could hear the deliberate insult behind Gideon's words? Probably, she acknowledged—no one else seemed aware of Gideon's antagonism towards her.

She turned back to him, chin raised as she met that challenge. 'What are your own feelings towards Christmas?'

They might have been the only two people in the room as they faced each other tensely.

Gideon's mouth quirked humourlessly. 'What do you think?'

He really didn't want to know what she was thinking about him right now.

'I have no idea,' she answered honestly. Trying to fathom the workings of Gideon could take a lifetime—and she really didn't have two minutes of her time to waste on the hateful man.

He grinned at her. 'I've always loved Christmas, too,' he told her mockingly.

It wasn't his words that disarmed her, but that grin. It transformed his whole face until he was boyish and charming. Two things she had never before associated with the arrogantly haughty Gideon Webber.

'Good,' she finally managed to answer inadequately.

The grin spread to the warmth of his dark blue eyes. 'Not what you expected to hear, was it?' he guessed shrewdly.

If there was one thing she had learnt about this man in the last twenty-four hours, it was never to expect the expected from him; he had so many facets to his nature it was impossible to second-guess anything he might do or say.

She gave a dismissive shrug. 'What I do or don't expect from you isn't really important, is it?' she dismissed heavily.

'Not to me, no,' he confirmed hardly.

Well, that definitely told you, didn't it, Molly? she acknowledged to herself ruefully. Just as well she felt the same way about him, wasn't it?

Brown eyes sparkled with sudden humour and she easily met his gaze this time. 'Well, I'm glad we got that out of the way, aren't you?' she taunted.

Was it her imagination or did she briefly see admiration flare in those dark blue eyes? Maybe, but it was so quickly masked by his usual mockery that even if she had seen it she knew Gideon wasn't happy with the emotion.

Well, that was just too bad. She was who she was, and she was pretty sure that wasn't the person Gideon thought she was. In fact, she was certain it wasn't!

Gideon glared down at her wordlessly for several seconds, eyes narrowing before he slowly turned away, an enigmatic smile curving those sculptured lips.

Now what? Molly found herself wondering for the second time in almost as many minutes. Why was it, she wondered, that this man always looked as if he knew something she didn't—like a cat that had lapped up all the cream?

And just as quickly she remonstrated with herself for such a fanciful thought; the only cat that Gideon Webber resembled was the feral kind—a hunting tiger, perhaps.

With her as his prey...

'We can all go out this afternoon and choose a fir

tree,' Sam was saying now. 'There's a place not far from here where you can pick and chop down your own,' he added with satisfaction.

'Excellent,' David said with obvious pleasure.

'A real traditional Christmas,' Gideon agreed, before once again looking at Molly, dark brows raised mockingly. 'Aren't you glad that Crys and Sam invited us all to stay over the holiday period?' he added softly.

Molly could feel all the colour draining from her face as the truth finally hit her with the force of an actual blow to the body. Neither David nor Gideon was leaving today. Or tomorrow. Or the day after. Or the day after that. These two men, as well as herself, were invited to spend Christmas at Falcon House, with Sam, Crys and Peter.

Why hadn't she guessed before? It had been there in front of her face all the time—the fact that David and Gideon had stayed the previous night, that neither man seemed in any hurry to leave this morning. Because they weren't leaving any time soon. In fact, it sounded as if the six of them were going to be cosily ensconced here together for the next four days at least!

'Still love Christmas?' a familiarly taunting voice murmured softly in the vicinity of her ear.

Her faith in the goodwill of Christmas had definitely been sorely tested in the last few minutes, but, yes, she still loved Christmas—in spite of whom she might be forced into sharing it with.

She turned sharply to tell Gideon as much, only to find that he was much closer than she had thought he was. His head bent towards hers, their breath intermingling as Molly's abrupt rejoinder died on her lips, and her gaze was held captive by Gideon's as her breathing seemed to stop altogether.

He really was the most attractive-looking man, that honey-blond hair falling endearingly over his forehead, his eyes a dark, fathomless blue over high cheekbones, the patrician nose and that firmly sculptured mouth.

'Will you be on the "naughty" or "nice" list this year, do you think?' he taunted softly.

Attractive-looking maybe. But as soon as he opened his mocking mouth the whole image was quickly dispelled.

Perhaps just as well…considering she had actually felt herself being drawn to that attraction for a few— mad—minutes.

She drew in a sharp breath. 'I…'

'Come on, you two,' David called over to them cheerily. 'We have decorations to get down from the attic,' he reminded them lightly.

Molly moved gratefully away from Gideon to join David as he followed Crys from the kitchen. But she was aware of Gideon's gaze following her every step of the way…

She was still muttering to herself as she tied the belt on her dressing gown later that evening, after taking a shower before going to bed.

Not that it had been an altogether bad day; the decorations had gone up without too much trouble, their evening meal had been prepared and eaten in companionably good humour, and conversation had flowed freely. Even after dinner, when they had all played a game of Monopoly, it hadn't been as bad as she had thought it was going to be—despite the fact that Gideon had easily been the winner.

No, on the surface it had been a successful day. Only

Molly, it seemed, had been aware of the barb behind every comment Gideon had made to her...

It had started with the naughty or nice remark, and continued unabated throughout the day—to such an extent that Molly had been relieved to excuse herself with the intention of taking a shower before going to bed.

'I'll give him naughty or nice,' she muttered to herself as she hurried down the hallway back to her bedroom. The last thing she wanted was to bump into Gideon when she was wearing only her dressing gown. No doubt he would find some sarcastic remark to make about that, too.

'I've always been nice,' she grumbled irritably as she opened her bedroom door.

Only to let out a loud scream as she saw someone silhouetted against the moonlight shining through her uncurtained window.

'I'm glad to hear it,' Gideon murmured dryly as he turned from gazing out of the window. 'But did you have to scream like that?' He gave a pained wince as he stepped forward into the glow of light given off by the bedside lamp she had left on for her return, still dressed in the casual shirt and trousers he had changed into earlier this evening.

'Yes, I had to scream like that!' Molly assured him furiously. 'What on earth do you think you're doing in my bedroom?' She glared across the room at him, her heart still beating double time, her legs feeling slightly shaky from the shock she had just received.

'Waiting for you, obviously,' he drawled dismissively. 'Do you think you could shut the bedroom door? If I'm staying, there's no point in drawing more attention to ourselves than necessary.'

No point in...! She had thought her torment was over

for at least today, and now he had the cheek to just appear in her bedroom like this!

Molly made no effort to close the door behind her. 'But you aren't staying,' she told him forcefully. 'In fact, I don't know what gave you the impression you could just come in here—'

'You said earlier we had to talk.' He shrugged.

Molly gave him an exasperated look. She *had* said they needed to talk—knew that he needed to be put right concerning several ideas he had conceived about her. But this was hardly the time—or the place—for such a discussion.

'Not now. And certainly not here,' she added impatiently. 'Do you have any idea what people are going to think if they find you in my bedroom?'

Crys, for one, would probably start picking out wedding-dress patterns.

'That was the reason I suggested you close the door,' Gideon reasoned dryly.

On second thought, maybe that wasn't such a bad idea, Molly decided, and she moved to close the door quietly. Anyone walking by to one of the bathrooms down the hallway would hear the two of them talking.

Gideon's brows were raised when she turned back to glare at him. 'Did you have a specific person in mind when you made that suggestion?' he taunted. 'I haven't interrupted an assignation, have I?'

Considering David was the only other eligible male in the household, Molly thought his remark in particularly bad taste. 'Don't judge everyone else by your own behaviour,' she snapped scornfully.

Gideon's eyes narrowed. 'Exactly what do you mean by that remark?' he demanded icily.

'Oh, it's different when it's made about you, isn't it?'

she derided exasperatedly, not really having any idea what she meant; it had just sounded like a good thing to say. It had also obviously touched a raw nerve...

'You—' She broke off abruptly as a knock sounded on the bedroom door, looking from the closed door to Gideon, her expression stricken.

'Molly?' Sam called concernedly through the door. 'I'm sorry to bother you, but Crys said she was sure she heard you scream a few minutes ago?'

Molly gave Gideon an accusing glare, having no idea what she should do now. If she opened the bedroom door then she would have no choice but to try to explain Gideon's presence here to Sam. And if she didn't open the door Sam was going to think it very odd.

'I think you had better open the door and reassure him of your safety,' Gideon murmured softly.

'Oh, you think, do you?' Molly muttered furiously. 'None of this would have happened at all if you had *thought* a little harder about the possible repercussions of a late-night visit to my bedroom!'

He gave a humourless smile. 'The only repercussion I could think of was if you thought I had come here with some idea of seduction in mind—'

'In your dreams, buster,' she cut in disgustedly.

'Molly...?' Sam sounded worried as he knocked a second time.

'It's okay, Sam.' Molly raised her voice so that he could hear her as she moved to open the door, deliberately keeping it only slightly ajar in the hope that he wouldn't be able to see Gideon in the room behind her. 'I'm fine, Sam,' she reassured brightly. 'I—it was just...I saw a spider.'

'And we all know how you love spiders,' her stepbrother sympathised affectionately. 'I'll come in and get rid of it for you,' he instantly offered.

Not with Gideon in her bedroom, he wouldn't! 'No, it's all right, Sam.' She firmly stood her ground in the doorway. 'I—you see…'

'The fact is, Sam—' Gideon spoke purposefully as he moved to stand visibly beside Molly '—I heard Molly scream, too, and I have already disposed of the spider by putting it out of the window.'

Molly closed her eyes briefly, wishing for this to simply be a nightmare, but knowing that it wasn't; it was possible to wake up from a nightmare! She opened her eyes again, to find Sam looking down at her speculatively, dark brows raised over knowing green eyes. After what Sam had told her earlier, concerning Crys's efforts at matchmaking, it wasn't too difficult to guess what he was thinking—or whose fault that was.

'That was kind of you, Gideon.' Sam turned his speculative gaze on the other man. 'I know from past experience how Molly hates to deal with spiders herself.'

'Didn't you know? Gideon is well known for his kindness.' Molly felt stung into snapping; the man wouldn't know 'kind' if it jumped up and bit him on the nose!

Her obvious sarcasm was completely wasted on Gideon. His expression was one of total unconcern.

'Well, if you're sure you're okay…?' Sam prompted lightly.

'I'm fine,' Molly assured him.

'I'll say good night, then.' Her stepbrother smiled, that knowing look still in his laughing green eyes.

'Again,' Gideon acknowledged dryly. 'I'll just have one last check for any more spiders before I leave,' he added dismissively.

And as there hadn't been a spider in the first place…

Molly found herself forcing a strained smile as Sam turned and walked back down the hallway to the bedroom he shared with Crys, giving him a half-hearted wave before closing her bedroom door and turning on Gideon.

'Now look what you've done!' she burst out furiously, eyes blazing deeply brown. 'Sam no more believes you were in my bedroom searching for non-existent spiders than I do!' she added accusingly.

He looked nonplussed and raised blond brows. 'He doesn't?'

'No,' she snapped, colour warming her cheeks as she remembered that earlier conversation with Sam. A conversation she had no intention of giving this man even a hint of!

Gideon shrugged unconcernedly. 'It sounded quite plausible to me. Especially as it turns out you really don't like spiders,' he added mockingly.

Molly's gaze narrowed dangerously. She had disliked spiders all her life, no matter what size they were. She had no explanation for it—knew there was no logic to the fear—she just couldn't stand them in the same room with her.

'So what do you imagine Sam *does* think I'm doing in your bedroom?' Gideon prompted softly, his expression deliberately guileless.

'I'm sure you can work that out for yourself!' she breathed agitatedly, knowing exactly what Sam would be thinking—saying—right now.

Gideon raised dark blond brows. 'As far as anyone else is concerned, we were introduced for the first time yesterday morning at the christening. Do you usually invite men into your bedroom on such short acquaintance?'

'Do I...? You're the one who invaded my bedroom, not the other way round!' she reminded accusingly.

It was bad enough that Sam and now Crys were aware that Gideon was in her bedroom, without having to take the responsibility for it, too. In fact, if she had to put up with any more of his insults this evening she was going to hit him.

'I didn't ''invade'' anywhere, Molly,' he came back evenly. 'I simply waited in here for you to come back from taking your shower.'

'And you had no right thinking you could do that,' she returned exasperatedly. 'I may have said the two of us need to talk, but I'm certainly in no mood to talk to you at the moment,' she added disgustedly.

There was a moment's silence, and Gideon's gaze was speculative now. 'Then what are you in the mood for?' he finally murmured softly.

Her eyes widened furiously at his obvious meaning. 'Why, you arrogant—'

'I don't think so.' Gideon reached out and easily caught her wrist as her hand would have made contact with one of his cheeks. 'In fact...' he muttered grimly, and his head lowered and his mouth took possession of hers.

Molly was so stunned by the unexpected kiss that for several long seconds she merely stood transfixed in his arms, his body hard against the softness of hers as his mouth explored hers with complete thoroughness.

Cold thoroughness...

That was what brought her to her senses, what stopped her from responding. Because, to her intense dismay, she actually wanted to respond.

Somewhere in the course of the last twenty-four hours—and she couldn't for the life of her imagine when it could have been—she had become attracted to Gideon Webber!

It couldn't have been when he was tormenting her. Nor when he was being sarcastic. After all, despite her earlier unfortunate love affair, she wasn't a complete masochist, and certainly hadn't deliberately allowed herself to become attracted to such an arrogantly impossible man. But for some reason she had done so anyway...

Which was why he had to stop kissing her!

'No!' She pulled sharply away to object, pushing away from him as his arms momentarily tightened about her.

Gideon looked down at her with hooded blue eyes. 'No?'

'No,' she repeated firmly, glaring up at him. 'I'm well aware of what you think of me, Gideon—'

'Are you?' he taunted, his arms dropping back to his sides as he slowly stepped away from her. 'Somehow I doubt that very much,' he added harshly.

Molly easily met that contemptuous gaze. 'I would have to be a complete idiot not to know,' she snapped. 'And, no matter what you may think to the contrary, I am not an idiot! For some reason you have decided I'm some sort of *femme fatale*—'

'For some reason?' he repeated scathingly, shaking his head disgustedly. 'I didn't imagine you that morning at James's apartment. Or the fact that you were completely naked underneath the shirt you were wearing— James's shirt,' he added pointedly. 'Two pretty good reasons for deciding something, wouldn't you say?' He eyed her contemptuously.

Molly gasped, could feel the flush in her cheeks. 'If taken at face value, yes. But—'

'What other way is there to take them?' Gideon cut in scornfully. 'You aren't trying to tell me that it was just coincidental that Crys was away at the time on a promotional tour for the publication of her newest cookery book?'

Molly looked at him wordlessly for several long seconds. He really did think...

She dropped down abruptly onto the bed, staring up at him disbelievingly. She knew he had a bad opinion of her, but...

She shook her head dazedly. 'Didn't you ever talk to James about that morning? Didn't you ask him?'

'No, I never spoke to James about it,' Gideon cut in harshly. 'And I didn't ask him anything, either. What I did do was tell him what an idiot he was for risking his marriage to Crys over a brief affair with someone like you,' he concluded grimly.

Molly felt numb—couldn't think, couldn't speak, could only stare at Gideon Webber in stunned disbelief. It had never occurred to her....

'So there you have it,' Gideon continued when she made no reply. 'Was this what you wanted when you suggested the two of us talk—all of this out in the open, with no more need for even cursory politeness between the two of us?'

'I wasn't aware that there had been much of that anyway,' Molly felt stung into replying, still stunned at what this man was accusing her of. He believed she'd had an affair with his brother James!

His mouth twisted humourlessly. 'There is in front of Crys and Sam,' he snapped. 'Crys obviously knows nothing about you and James—'

'There *was* no me and James!' she cried protestingly, at the same time knowing that on the evidence this man had, her protest sounded hollow, to say the least. Even if it *was* the truth.

His top lip curled contemptuously. 'Obviously nothing James felt important enough to need to make any deathbed confession to Crys.' Gideon gave a disgusted shake of his head. 'That's something to be grateful for, at least!'

'But…'

'But I know. And you know,' Gideon continued hardly. 'Let's just leave it at that, hmm?'

Molly's eyes widened disbelievingly. 'You surely don't think that I would ever—'

'Who knows what you're capable of?' he cut in disgustedly. 'From what I can gather, Crys is your best friend—and yet you felt no compunction about taking advantage of her absence from the marital home to jump into bed with her husband.'

This was incredible. Unbelievable. Oh, it certainly went a long way towards explaining Gideon's behaviour towards her—it was just totally inaccurate as to what had really happened just over three years ago.

'There's only one positive thing that I can see about this situation,' Gideon continued hardly.

'There's a positive to all this?' Molly echoed dazedly.

'Oh, yes.' Gideon nodded with grim satisfaction.

She blinked. 'And that would be…?'

Those dark blue eyes gleamed with that same satisfaction. 'Crys is now married to your stepbrother. A situation that would certainly alter if you were ever to feel the need to clear your own conscience. Crys would find it very difficult to stay married to the brother of the woman who had an affair with her first husband.'

'Now just a minute—'

'I've wasted all the time that I'm going to tonight,' Gideon rasped with a dismissive shake of his head.

On her, that was, Molly acknowledged numbly. This was worse, so much worse than she could ever have imagined. Oh, she had known there had to be a reason behind Gideon's complete contempt for her, had guessed that it probably had something to do with finding her in James's apartment that morning just over three years ago, but she had never imagined...

'Be warned, Molly,' Gideon added harshly. 'I won't ever let you do or say anything that will hurt Crys. Is that understood?' he prompted determinedly.

She swallowed hard. 'Perfectly.' She nodded, wondering if he weren't being just a little hypocritical. His protectiveness of Crys—erroneous as it might be in her own case—seemed to indicate more than just ex-brother-in-law affection on his own part.

Not that she was particularly interested in that; it was his belief of her own behaviour that was so disturbing.

Crys had been, and still was, Molly's best friend. And Molly had known James for some time before introducing Crys to him; James had been one of her best friends, too. But that was all he had ever been: her friend.

Not that she thought this man was about to believe that for a moment. He had formed an opinion of her on one brief meeting. A bad opinion. And the only way to even try to explain herself was to give him an explanation of a time in her life she would rather forget. An explanation he was unlikely to believe in any case.

'Good,' Gideon bit out with satisfaction. 'In that case, I have nothing further to say to you. Except—'

'Please,' Molly protested weakly, putting up a shaking hand to the temple that had started to throb pain-fully. 'I've already heard enough of your insults for one evening.' She sighed heavily.

Gideon paused on his way to the bedroom door. 'Oh, I wasn't about to insult you again, Molly,' he assured her lightly.

'No?' she said disbelievingly.

'No,' he said derisively. 'I was about to tell you that I'd lied about dealing with the spider. It's on the ceiling directly above your head. Have a good night!' he added tauntingly, before letting himself out of the bedroom.

Molly didn't see him leave. One glance at the ceiling above her head revealed that there was indeed a spider. A huge one!

She shot off the bed so fast she almost fell over, staring in horrified fascination at the long-legged, fat-bodied insect.

Swine!

Rotter!

Sadist!

And she wasn't referring to the spider!

CHAPTER FOUR

THE phrase 'you look like hell' came to mind as Molly looked at herself in the dressing-table mirror the following morning. Her hair stood out in a wild tumble of curls and her face pale, with dark shadows beneath her eyes.

It wasn't just any morning, either; it was Christmas Eve.

But she had never felt less like Christmas than she did at this moment. She had spent a sleepless night, alternately looking at the spider or thinking of the things Gideon had said to her the previous evening.

He really believed she'd had an affair with his brother James behind Crys's back.

For one thing, she hadn't felt that way about James— had only ever looked on him as a friend. For another, Crys was her best friend; there was no way Molly could ever have betrayed that friendship, even if she had been in love with James, by sneaking behind Crys's back and having an affair with him.

But if Gideon ever chose to tell Crys of that morning when he had arrived at the apartment Crys had shared with James, and found Molly in residence, her only clothing one of James's shirts, would her friend be able to believe in her complete innocence?

Molly would assure her that James had only ever been her friend. But in light of that night Molly had once spent at the married couple's apartment, while

53

Crys had been away, the night Gideon was aware of, too, would Crys still believe in her innocence?

Gideon had contemptuously assured her he had no intention of ever telling Crys about that night, that he had no desire to hurt her or to ever see her hurt, but would he continue to feel that way if it no longer suited his own plans?

Unhappily, the conclusion Molly had come to during the long sleepless night had been that she simply didn't know the answer to that question. Despite her aversion to going anywhere near the man ever again, she would have to speak to Gideon on the subject.

But not until she had done something about the way she looked.

And she did try. She washed her hair and styled it until it was silkily gleaming on her shoulders, applied make-up to hide her paleness and those dark shadows beneath her eyes, even chose her clothes carefully: a burnt-orange-coloured blouse teamed with fitted black denims. It was just that none of those things could hide the fact that she looked and felt thoroughly exhausted from all the thinking she had done during the night.

Oh, damn the man—and his suspicious mind. If it weren't for both those things she would be enjoying a warm family Christmas with Crys, Sam and the baby, just as she had envisaged when she'd accepted their invitation to stay.

'Last again?' Gideon taunted the moment she entered the kitchen, shortly after nine o'clock.

He *would* have to be the first person she saw this morning—and he wasn't alone, either. Crys was sitting at the kitchen table with him.

The latter turned to smile warmly at Molly as she walked over to pour herself some coffee from the pot.

'Sam and David have taken Peter and Merlin for a walk to give me a few minutes' break; Peter was cranky all night—didn't seem to want to settle.' She grimaced affectionately.

'I know the feeling.' Molly nodded, sipping her hot coffee, her brooding gaze daring Gideon to come back with another one of his barbed comments after the total inaccuracy of his initial statement; they both knew that David had been the last down the previous morning.

Crys at once looked concerned. 'Sam said there was a spider in your bedroom last night,' she sympathised.

Molly looked coldly at Gideon now. 'There was,' she confirmed flatly. And that sadistic swine had left her alone in her bedroom with it all night.

He returned her gaze steadily, the blandness of his expression giving away none of his emotions or thoughts.

In Molly's opinion he didn't have any of the former, and far too much of the latter.

'Lucky that Gideon was able to deal with it for you.' Crys nodded happily.

The only thing Gideon had dealt with was his own need to tell Molly exactly what he thought of her— before leaving her alone with that monster spider!

'Wasn't it?' she returned noncommittally, no longer even looking at Gideon, just too tired to cope with any more of his scorn, even in a look. 'Could I borrow your car to go into town this morning?' She turned to Crys. 'I still have a little last-minute shopping to do.'

It had also occurred to her some time during the sleepless night that, as she hadn't known they were going to be here over the holiday period, she didn't have presents to give to either David or Gideon tomorrow morning.

Not that she particularly wanted to get Gideon a Christmas present, unless it was a bottle of arsenic, but it would certainly look odd if she bought something for everyone else and deliberately excluded him.

There was no help for it; she would have to buy him a present, too. Something completely impersonal, she had finally decided—like a one-way ticket to the North Pole. He would certainly feel at home there, amongst all that ice and snow.

'I'm driving into town myself this morning.' Gideon was the one to answer her. 'So you may as well come in with me.'

Molly's eyes widened in horror at the thought of spending any more time alone with this man while she felt so tired and vulnerable. And she made no effort to hide the emotion when he looked at her mockingly.

'What a wonderful idea!' Thankfully Crys had turned to look at Gideon and didn't see Molly's response to the suggestion. 'Perhaps you wouldn't mind picking up a newspaper and my order from the butcher's while you're there?'

'Glad to,' Gideon assured her smoothly.

'Great.' Crys grinned as she stood up. 'I'll just go and get the list.' She hurried from the room.

Oh, yes, just great, Molly echoed heavily in her thoughts, knowing it had been taken for granted that she would accept Gideon's offer to drive her into town.

And why not? Ordinarily it would be the normal thing to do. It was just that there was nothing in the least 'ordinary' about the emotions that passed like electric volts between Gideon and herself.

'You look tired this morning.'

It was a statement, not a question, and a totally unwelcome one as far as Molly was concerned. Once again she looked up to glare at Gideon. 'And whose fault is that, do you think?' she challenged tartly.

He grimaced. 'From the accusation in your tone, I gather that it's mine...?'

Her eyes flashed deeply brown. 'You gather correctly. You—'

'Here we are.' Crys bustled back into the room with the appropriate list. 'It's the shop in the square—not the one down the street,' she added lightly, not seeming in the least aware of the tension in the kitchen between Molly and Gideon.

And why should she be? Molly reasoned ruefully. As Gideon had already pointed out, as far as any of the family were concerned the two of them had only met for the first time at the christening.

'I'm sure that between the two of us we'll manage to find it,' Gideon assured her as he stood up. 'Hmm, Molly?' he prompted pointedly.

Molly felt a small shock run through her body as he called her by her first name, sure that it was the first time he had done so in the last two days. Not that it had sounded in the least warm or familiar—just slightly alien coming from this particular man.

'I'm sure we will,' she confirmed flatly. 'I'll just go and get my coat and meet you at the car.' She turned to leave without waiting for any response to this remark, just needing to get away for a few minutes on her own.

To regroup.

Also to make sure she removed all sharp instruments from her handbag—just in case she was goaded into sticking any of them into Gideon as he drove. After all, it was him she felt like doing harm to, not herself.

The green Jaguar saloon was comfortable, she would give him that, Molly allowed grudgingly a few minutes later when she sat beside Gideon as he drove the car down the long driveway out onto the public road. Warm and comfortable. But that was only the car. The owner was anything but those things.

Perhaps it was too warm and comfortable, she decided a few minutes later as her eyes began to close and her head to nod tiredly.

'You really are tired, aren't you?' Gideon said slowly as Molly made a concerted effort to stay awake.

'Why would I say I was if I wasn't?' she snapped back testily.

There was complete silence in the car for several long seconds, and then Gideon gave a sigh. 'Perhaps I was a little hard on you last night,' he said grudgingly.

Molly turned to give him a sharply suspicious look. Surely he couldn't be apologising for the things he had accused her of yesterday evening?

He glanced at her, dark blond brows rising as she warily returned his brief gaze before it returned to the road ahead. 'I was referring to my omission to dispose of the spider,' he drawled derisively.

No, she had been right the first time; he wasn't apologising for the accusations he had made.

'Did you spend all night keeping a wary eye on it?' he added with some amusement—completely nullifying the previous apology.

'Don't give it another thought,' Molly dismissed hardly, determined not to give him the satisfaction of knowing she had done just that.

'I wouldn't have done—' he shrugged '—if it weren't for the fact that you look so exhausted this morning.'

'By "exhausted" I presume you mean awful?' she bit out resentfully; so much for the washed hair and make-up.

He gave another shrug of those broad shoulders. 'Well...'

Molly felt the angry colour warm her cheeks as she glared at him. 'Do you ever say anything nice?' she snapped caustically.

'Frequently.' He nodded, completely unabashed. 'For instance, in contrast to what you were wearing on Sunday, the blouse you're wearing this morning suits your colouring perfectly.'

The compliment was so unexpected that it left Molly speechless. And slightly tearful, she realised with dismay.

Overtired.

Overwrought.

Just over-everything...

Gideon gave her another glance, frowning slightly. 'Wasn't that a nice thing to say?'

Molly gave a deep sigh, aware even as she did so of just how tensely she had been sitting as she relaxed back against the seat. The problem was, even 'nice' sounded suspect coming from this man.

'Thank you,' she accepted huskily.

'You're welcome.' He nodded. 'I'll go and hunt down the spider when we get back, if you like,' he added huskily.

She shook her head wearily. 'There's no need for that.'

His eyes widened. 'You managed to deal with it yourself?'

'No,' she acknowledged ruefully. 'I meant that to my certain knowledge it hasn't moved an inch from its balancing act above the bed—so there will be no need to hunt it down.'

A frown appeared between those dark blue eyes. 'I'm not usually a deliberately vindictive man,' he rasped.

Molly grimaced. 'You're just happy to make me the exception, hmm?'

The frown deepened. 'Not happy, exactly...'

'Oh, just go for it, Gideon.' Molly gave a tiredly rueful laugh.

The frown remained. 'You really spent all night watching that spider?'

'I really did.' She nodded self-derisively. 'After all, I could hardly go along and ask Sam for help after you had assured him so emphatically that you had already dealt with it.'

Gideon's mouth thinned. 'I feel really bad now,' he rasped self-disgustedly.

Molly eyed him questioningly. 'How bad?'

'Bad,' he accepted slowly.

'Bad enough to listen to my side of what happened three years ago?' Molly came back, more decisively than she would have believed herself capable of this particular morning.

He stiffened. 'No,' he rasped harshly. 'I feel guilty for leaving that spider in your room when you obviously are an arachnophobic. That doesn't mean I'm about to let you try to convince me that I didn't see that morning what I definitely did see.'

Hard. Unyielding. Judgemental, Molly decided frustratedly. How could she reason with a man like that?

She couldn't, came the unpleasant answer. Although that wasn't going to stop her from trying.

'However,' Gideon continued hardly before she could formulate a reply, 'what I am willing to do is call a truce on the subject over the Christmas period.'

'Big of you!' she snapped impatiently.

His mouth tightened ominously. 'It's the best offer you're going to get,' he bit out harshly. 'In fact,' he continued grimly, 'as far as I'm concerned it's the only offer you're going to get.'

In other words, take it or leave it! And in the circumstances—not wanting to spoil Christmas for the others, if any of them should pick up on the barbed warfare between herself and Gideon—Molly knew she would have to take it.'

Her mouth twisted humourlessly. 'I take it this "truce" will cease being in effect the moment midnight strikes on Boxing Night?'

His own smile was just as humourless. 'Actually, I'm staying until the morning of the twenty-eighth—think you can manage to be polite for that long?' He quirked dark blond brows at her.

'I'm not the one being impolite!' she returned waspishly.

Gideon gave a shrug of broad shoulders. 'I'm willing to give the alternative a try.'

Molly bit back the angry retort she would have liked to make, on the basis that it wasn't a very good way to begin a truce—but that didn't mean she didn't still have murderous tendencies towards this arrogant man.

'Fine,' she bit out between gritted teeth.

He turned to give her a mocking glance. 'So, what are you going to buy me for Christmas?' he taunted.

Molly's eyes widened at his astuteness in guessing what her 'last-minute shopping' actually was, and then she gave a rueful shake of her head. 'I did have a bottle of arsenic in mind—but then I decided that might be a little too obvious!'

To her surprise. Gideon gave an appreciative chuckle. And once again it transformed his whole face, giving him a boyish look, turning his blue gaze warm rather than arctic.

Which, considering Molly's total awareness of him probably wasn't a good idea...

'Maybe a little,' he finally conceded, still smiling.

'What would you like me to get you?' she prompted interestedly, having no idea what this man's interests or preferences were.

In any subject!

He was here alone, so he obviously wasn't involved in a relationship at the moment; he would be spending Christmas with whoever it was if that were the case. But that posed the question: what sort of woman was he attracted to? Obviously not petite redheads who happened to be frightened of spiders.

Now why on earth had she had that thought? Molly wondered crossly. It was bad enough that she should have allowed herself to be attracted to him, without wishing he might find some redeeming attraction in her.

Besides, she already had an idea that Gideon's attraction lay towards fragile silver-blonds with haunting grey eyes. Crys...

'Well, I don't like chocolate, and I have enough aftershave already,' Gideon answered her slowly. 'Would a book be impersonal enough, do you think?' he prompted softly.

Molly felt her cheeks flush; did this man know everything? 'I'm sure that it would,' she bit out tersely. 'What sort of book did you have in mind?' Something erudite and learned, no doubt, Molly reasoned wryly.

Gideon shrugged. 'There is a book I've been meaning to buy for some time. I was waiting for it to come out in paperback, and then I just forgot to buy it...'

'Yes?' Molly prompted dryly, wondering if her bank

account had enough in it to cover the cost of a book this man hadn't yet got around to buying for himself.

The move from America back to England had worked out quite expensive, what with shipping her few personal belongings back here and finding herself a flat to live in. But, on the bright side, at least she was one of the ten per cent of actors who were in work at any one time.

Gideon eyed her frowningly. 'Perhaps you already had something in mind? Besides the arsenic, that is,' he taunted.

She gave a shake of her head. 'Not a thing.' She doubted the one-way ticket to the North Pole would have been any better received. 'In fact, I would more than welcome any useful advice you could give me in that direction,' she assured him briskly, knowing she had no idea what to get for David, either.

She was also wondering what Gideon had got *her* for Christmas...

Obviously he had already known he would be staying for Christmas, and who the other guests were to be, so he would have purchased something for each of them before coming up to Yorkshire. Knowing how he felt about her, she dreaded to think what he would have as a gift for her.

Gideon nodded. 'Okay, then. One of my favourite comedians is Billy Connolly, and—'

'I don't believe it!' Molly protested incredulously, and colour flooded her cheeks as she realised what she had said. 'I mean—well...Billy Connolly is—' Whatever she had been trying to say, she gave it up as a bad job to stare at Gideon dazedly.

Billy Connolly? He was her absolute all-time favourite comedian, and had proved himself to be an ex-

ceptional actor in recent years, too. She would just
never, ever have thought that Gideon Webber would
like him, too…

'An acquired taste,' Gideon acknowledged dryly, obviously mistaking her surprise for censure. 'One that I
acquired during my university days and have never
lost,' he added ruefully.

Molly had already read the book Gideon was referring to, written by the comedian's wife, and had found
it to be moving, tragic. But ultimately the often outra-
geous Scottish comedian's gift of humour had shone
through all the hardships suffered in his childhood. She
was just having difficulty coming to terms with having
that like shared by Gideon Webber, of all people.

'One that I acquired years ago, too,' Molly told him
evenly, deliberately masking her surprise at his preference. If asked, she would have sworn that she and
Gideon had absolutely nothing in common. 'And it's a
great book,' she assured him. 'What do you think I
should get David?' She deliberately changed the subject, still slightly rattled by discovering that she and
Gideon had the same sense of humour.

'That's easy,' Gideon answered smilingly. 'We discussed the book last night, and David hasn't read it yet,
either.'

David sharing her slightly offbeat sense of humour
she could more readily understand…

Although wasn't it just a little too impersonal to buy
both men the same gift? It might look as if she had
been out and bought a job lot to attain a discount.

Gideon glanced at her. 'I can assure you that we will
both be more than pleased with the gift.'

'Fine with me,' Molly accepted briskly, deciding that
impersonal was definitely the way to go with both these

men when taking into account Sam's warning of Crys's attempts at matchmaking.

Something to keep constantly in mind, considering Crys's satisfied look as she'd stood in the driveway and watched the two of them drive off together earlier.

CHAPTER FIVE

'THERE we are,' Gideon told Molly with satisfaction as he turned from putting the huge spider out of her bedroom window.

'Thank you,' she accepted awkwardly, finding his presence in her bedroom for the second time in twenty-four hours more than a little disconcerting.

Their trip into town together hadn't turned out quite as she had expected. She had thought that Gideon would go off and do his own chores while she wandered around doing her own. But that hadn't happened at all—Gideon seeming quite happy to stroll around with her. Even when she'd gone into the bookshop to buy the two books Gideon had simply waited outside for her, and then they had recommenced their stroll up the street.

It had been a little disconcerting, to say the least. The shoppers around them had obviously been infused with the happiness of the Christmas spirit, and there had been none of the mad rush and bustle in this little country town that Molly had left behind her in London. People had seemed to have time to stop and chat with each other, even though most of them were laden down with gaily wrapped parcels, and the coloured lights and decorated windows had all added to the relaxed atmosphere of warmth and cheer.

Surrounded by such obvious good humour and good-will, it had been impossible not to become caught up in it—even Gideon had seemed more relaxed, if not exactly friendly.

That was probably a little too much to hope for, Molly accepted ruefully.

But his slightly softened attitude certainly gave her hope that the Christmas holiday wasn't going to be as unpleasant as she had thought it would—but not enough to introduce the subject of that night just over three years ago; that would be sure to reintroduce a complete dampener on the whole thing.

'Where do you suppose everyone is?' Molly frowned now, anxious to get Gideon out of her bedroom, but also concerned that there had seemed to be no one else at home when they'd arrived back a short time ago, having picked up the requested newspaper and meat from the butcher's.

Gideon shrugged. 'Maybe they've all gone out for lunch on the assumption we would probably do the same?'

Oh, yes, she could just see Gideon and herself sitting down to eat lunch alone together—something guaranteed to give them both indigestion, she would have thought.

Although, bearing in mind Crys's newly acquired matchmaking tendencies, Molly wouldn't put it past her friend to have deliberately left her alone here with Gideon in an effort to further their friendship.

'Maybe.' She grimaced. 'In that case—'

'Hi, you two!' David greeted them from the hallway just outside Molly's bedroom. 'Do you happen to know whether or not you've had chickenpox?'

'I beg your pardon?' Gideon frowned uncomprehendingly.

'Sorry?' Molly felt just as puzzled—although that

didn't stop the colour entering her cheeks at Gideon once again being found in her bedroom.

David stepped into the doorway. 'Apparently the reason Peter has been feeling less than his usual cheerful self is due to a rash on his face and chest. The doctor is with him now, deciding whether or not it's chickenpox,' he explained with a grimace.

'Oh, no,' Molly groaned sympathetically.

'Chickenpox?' Gideon's frown deepened. 'Isn't he a little young to get something like that?'

Too young, Molly acknowledged worriedly. Peter was only three months old…

'That's what the doctor said,' David acknowledged lightly.

'I'll go and see Crys now…'

David put out a hand to stop Molly as she would have hurried from the bedroom. 'Not if you haven't already had chickenpox,' he warned.

'I have,' she assured him. 'According to my mother I had every childhood disease going before I was a year old,' she added ruefully.

'Why am I not surprised?' Gideon muttered dryly.

Her eyes flashed deeply brown as she shot him a look across the room. 'Have *you* had chickenpox?'

He drew his breath in with a heavy sigh. 'As it happens, no,' he admitted with a grimace.

'Oops,' David sympathised. 'If it actually is chickenpox, it seems that Peter will have been at his most infectious from the christening onwards,' he explained at Gideon's questioningly raised brows.

It was all Molly could do to hold back her smile. Oh, it would be awful if a baby as young as Peter had contracted the infection, but the thought of the arrogantly confident Gideon Webber struck down with the unsightly rash was enough to make anyone smile.

'Perhaps you should leave now?' she suggested lightly—hope still sprang eternal that this man might not be here to ruin Christmas.

'That wouldn't be allowed, I'm afraid,' David was the one to answer her. 'The doctor has already said that if it is chickenpox, if we've all been in contact with Peter during the last forty-eight hours, that we would have to remain a self-contained unit for at least the next five days or so to see if any of us develop the infection.'

Five days? When Molly had been expecting to rid herself of Gideon within a couple of days!

But the look of mockery that had replaced Gideon's frown was enough for her to immediately hide her dismay. 'I'll go and see if there's any news,' she offered briskly, deliberately turning away from Gideon—and his knowingly taunting look.

Poor Peter did look very disgruntled when Molly entered the nursery a few seconds later, his face all red and blotchy from crying. Crys's face was pale and anxious as she held him in her arms.

'How is he?' Molly asked a grey-faced Sam as he stood beside Crys, looking down worriedly at his young son.

'It's what's commonly called milk rash.' It was the young female doctor who answered her lightly. 'Uncomfortable for Peter, but fortunately he doesn't have a temperature or anything like that,' she added reassuringly. 'Poor little love is just feeling a trifle fed up with the world—aren't you, Peter?' She touched him comfortingly. 'And his first Christmas, too.'

In actual fact, apart from the slight rash on his face and chest, and his cheeks blotchy from crying, Peter looked in better health than either of his parents, Molly decided, after taking in Crys's ashen face and Sam's anxious gaze as he continued to look at his wife and son.

'Well, that's really good news.' Molly smiled at the pretty doctor.

The doctor grinned back. 'Isn't it?' She nodded, obviously relieved to have someone other than worried parents to talk to. 'I'm sure the rash will fade very soon, and Peter will be back to his normal placid self,' she added dismissively, 'but if you have any more worries about him at all over Christmas, please don't hesitate to call me. I shall be on call all over the holiday period,' she said ruefully.

'Poor you,' Molly sympathised as she escorted the doctor out of the nursery and down the wide staircase to the front door.

The lights on the Christmas tree they had dressed the previous evening blinked on and off warmly as they passed the sitting-room.

The doctor shrugged. 'It seems only fair, as my partners all have families they would like to be with.'

The doctor was probably aged in her mid-thirties, and was extremely pretty in a blond, blue-eyed, no-nonsense sort of way; it seemed unfair that she was to spend Christmas alone.

'Everything okay?' David prompted as he came out of the sitting-room. He was obviously the one responsible for putting on the Christmas lights; neither Crys nor Sam was in any mood to think of anything to do with Christmas at the moment.

Molly drifted off into the kitchen as the doctor and the actor fell into easy conversation and David took over the task of escorting the doctor to her car.

From the looks of things, what with Peter's obvious discomfort and the doctor's visit, no one had yet had any lunch, and now certainly wasn't the time to ask Crys what she'd had in mind for the meal. But a quick look in the fridge revealed a huge bowl of freshly made chicken soup, and Molly had already seen there were three French sticks on the table to accompany it.

'Oh!' She gasped as she straightened from the fridge to find Gideon standing behind her; he moved with the silence of a feline.

'Steady.' He reached out and took the heavy bowl from her as it wobbled precariously. 'Where shall I put this?'

Those raised blond brows dared her to make the answer that had sprung so readily to her lips, but Molly clamped those lips together for several seconds before answering. 'Just on the table, thanks,' she said briskly. 'I think Crys and Sam need to eat something after all that worry,' she added ruefully.

Gideon nodded. 'Nothing ever looks as bad on a full stomach.'

Molly wasn't so sure that a bowl of soup and some French bread would work the same magic with her, concerning spending Christmas with this man.

Gideon grinned as he seemed to guess her thoughts. 'Well...usually not,' he drawled mockingly.

She glared up at him. 'Why don't you lay the table and make yourself useful, instead of standing there tormenting me?' she bit out crossly, having transferred the soup to a large saucepan and put it on top of the Aga to warm while she cut the bread up into more manageable pieces.

Gideon didn't move, still standing far too close to her

than was comfortable. 'Am I tormenting you?' he murmured huskily.

Molly swallowed hard. 'You know that you are!' she snapped, at the same time knowing that her voice lacked conviction.

What was it about this man that made her so aware of him? So physically aware of him—totally aware of the muscled tautness of his body, of the clean, male smell of him, of the arrogant curve to that sculptured mouth. In fact, she was so much aware of him at the moment that she could hardly breathe, let alone force her limbs to move away from him.

That dark blue gaze easily held her captive. 'In what way am I tormenting you?' he prompted softly, the warmth of his breath stirring the silky tendrils of hair at her temple, his mouth only inches away from her own now as he bent his head towards hers.

In what way was he tormenting her? In *every* way. Verbally, he more often than not left her self-confidence in shreds. Emotionally, he reduced her to a jibbering wreck. And as for physically...

She didn't want to think about what Gideon did to her physically.

'I must say it's good that Peter doesn't have chickenpox after all,' David said with relief as he strolled into the kitchen.

Molly looked up wordlessly at Gideon for several more long seconds, unable to break the pull of that darkly compelling gaze. She felt her cheeks pale as the seconds passed, knowing Gideon was the last man she should ever have allowed to affect her in this way.

Why did he?

He was rude to her. Insulted her at every opportunity.

Believed her capable of practising deceit on her best friend. Added to which, she didn't even like him.

But as he continued to look at her she could barely breathe, let alone think straight. Not a good combination.

'Oh, good—lunch,' David murmured with satisfaction as he gazed in at the warming soup.

Molly dragged her gaze away from Gideon's with effort, turning to smile at the other man. 'Perhaps one of you would like to tell Crys and Sam that lunch will be ready soon?' she suggested lightly, able to step away from Gideon now that she wasn't held captive by that compelling gaze. 'I know Peter isn't feeling so good, but they still need to eat,' she added ruefully.

'I'll go,' Gideon offered. 'I can always stay upstairs with Peter while they come down and eat, if they have a problem with leaving him alone.'

Molly looked across at him. 'That's kind of you,' she murmured slowly.

He paused in the doorway. 'I can be kind,' he assured her hardly, before striding purposefully from the room.

Molly grimaced her dismay, knowing she had once again said the wrong thing. But she knew, in their present circumstances, she would be hard-pressed to say the right thing where Gideon was concerned.

'Lovers' tiff?'

She turned sharply to frown at David as he stood watching her, a teasing smile curving his lips, dark brows raised mockingly.

He shrugged at her obvious displeasure. 'Sam said something this morning about Gideon coming to your rescue last night concerning a spider in your bedroom. Then the two of you went off shopping together earlier. And he was in your bedroom a few minutes ago,' he reasoned, his smile widening at her look of obvious displeasure. 'What else am I supposed to think?'

'Not what you *are* thinking,' she snapped disgruntledly.

'No?' David speculated.

'No!' she bit out frustratedly, a rueful smile starting to curve her lips now. 'Last night. This morning. In my bedroom just now. This is all just some silly idea of Crys's... I suppose you do realise that this is all some mistaken matchmaking on Crys's part? And you're another prime candidate?' She turned the tables on him, knowing she had scored a point when he looked totally stunned.

'Me?' David was visibly dumbfounded. 'But I thought Gideon...? Who does Crys have picked out for me, then?' he said dazedly.

'Me,' Molly drawled. 'According to Sam, she isn't too bothered as to whether it's Gideon or you I become involved with, so long as it's someone!'

'Thanks!' David grimaced.

'You're welcome.' She grinned, enjoying his discomfort after his having teased her so mercilessly.

He frowned. 'And I thought Crys was just being kind by inviting me to stay for Christmas!'

'Oh, she was,' Molly instantly assured him. 'She is. Crys is one of the nicest people you could ever hope to meet.'

'I'm glad we're all agreed on that point at least,' Gideon rasped as he returned to the kitchen, dark gaze narrowed questioningly as he looked stonily at Molly.

She held that gaze for several long seconds, and then she looked away, knowing from Gideon's accusing look exactly what he was thinking. But it was impossible to defend herself against such ingrained prejudice. And with David in the room she had no intention of even trying to do so.

Besides, Gideon, at least, was unaware of Crys's attempts at matchmaking. And Molly wanted him to remain that way.

'Are they coming down to join us?' she prompted distantly.

'Sam is,' Gideon confirmed. 'Crys will have something later; she's going to stay upstairs and have a nap with Peter. After her disturbed night, and with the relief of knowing it's nothing serious, she probably needs sleep more than food at the moment,' he added affectionately.

Molly knew how Crys felt. Her own night had been far from restful. Although she didn't have the added worry over Peter to contend with, too.

She nodded. 'I'll go and take over from her later, so she can have something to eat.'

Gideon eyed her for several seconds. 'That's kind of you,' he finally murmured dryly.

Deliberately. Mockingly. Tauntingly.

Okay, so neither of them had a particularly good opinion of the other. But if they continued like this it was going to make this time more difficult for the others than it already was.

'My mother always told me that kindness is a virtue,' she dismissed lightly, beginning to serve soup into four bowls.

'So is loyalty,' Gideon rasped harshly.

Molly stiffened, knowing exactly where that remark was directed. 'And honesty,' she bit out tautly, brown gaze challenging his now.

'Hey, can anyone join in this conversation? Or is this just some private thing between the two of you?' David interjected dryly, drawing their attention to the fact that he was still in the room.

It was a fact both of them seemed to have momentarily forgotten in their antagonism towards each other, Molly acknowledged, and she shot David a rueful smile.

'Luncheon is served,' she announced decisively, turning to smile at Sam as he came into the room. 'Are they okay?' she prompted gently.

He grimaced. 'Fine.' He nodded. 'But this was the very last thing we needed on top of… Well, we could definitely have done without this at the moment,' he muttered tensely.

Molly frowned at him. 'On top of what…?' she prompted, hoping the discord between herself and Gideon wasn't becoming a problem for the others.

'Nothing,' Sam dismissed abruptly. 'Just forget I said anything,' he muttered, sitting down to eat his soup distractedly.

'But Diana—Dr Chisholm,' David corrected ruefully at their puzzled looks. 'She told me that she doesn't foresee any complications with Peter.'

'I'm sure there won't be.' Sam nodded. 'I'm just worried about Crys, that's all.' He shrugged. 'She looks on our marriage, and Peter's birth, as her second chance. I don't want anything to spoil that. Not that it will,' he added hurriedly.

'What could possibly happen to spoil it for you?' Molly looked at her stepbrother dazedly.

'Exactly—what could?' Gideon was the one to answer hardly.

Molly didn't look up from her soup, but nevertheless she sensed his censorious gaze on her. And the reason for it.

So shopping this morning, even getting rid of that

spider from her bedroom earlier, had just been a temporary respite after all; Gideon obviously still totally distrusted her where Crys's happiness was concerned.

And not only was his distrust totally unwarranted, it was also highly insulting.

It also brought into question—once again—Gideon's own feelings towards Crys...

CHAPTER SIX

'I'M JUST going into town to pick up a few things Crys forgot to get.' David told them shortly after lunch. 'Anyone fancy coming for a drive with me?'

Sam had gone back upstairs to sit with Crys and Peter, taking some soup and bread up on a tray for his wife, leaving Molly with very little to do this afternoon apart from wrapping those two extra Christmas presents—which certainly wasn't going to take very long— and, of course, providing Gideon with a convenient target to vent his sarcastic humour on.

'You go ahead, Molly,' he invited now, barely glancing up from the newspaper he was reading as he sat at the kitchen table. 'I'll stay here in case Sam and Crys need anything.'

Her cheeks flushed angrily; as if she needed his permission to do anything. Or to be made to feel guilty because she felt the need to get outside in the fresh air— away from him—for a while.

'What the…?' Gideon rasped before Molly could think of a suitably cutting reply to his sarcasm, his attention suddenly riveted on the newspaper he had merely been glancing through before.

'What is it?' Molly frowned at him worriedly.

'Hmm,' David murmured distractedly, having glanced over Gideon's shoulder at the newspaper. 'It's a good photograph of us all, but…'

'Exactly—but!' Gideon muttered angrily, standing up, with the newspaper now tightly gripped between his hands. 'I don't think either Sam or Crys are going to like this.' He frowned darkly.

'What is it?' Molly repeated agitatedly, moving to look at the newspaper herself now.

What she saw there made her breath catch in her throat.

The christening on Sunday had been a completely private family and friends affair, but the photograph in this newspaper meant that at least one member of the press had found out about it. Not only had they found out about it, they had obviously hidden somewhere and taken a photograph of them all as they were leaving the church. The proud parents stood in the midst of Gideon, David and Molly, and all of them were named in the caption beneath the photograph...

'Oh, no!' Molly gasped her dismay, knowing exactly how much Sam was going to hate this.

Twelve years ago his life had been made a living hell because of his ex-fiancée and the lies she had told the press about him, to the extent that he had chosen to hide himself away here in the wilds of Yorkshire. His marriage to Crys almost two years ago had helped to soften his attitude, but certainly not to the extent that he would be happy to have his photograph plastered all over the newspapers. Or that of his newborn son...

'Damn it,' Gideon muttered grimly. 'Why the hell can't they leave them alone?'

'Because it's news.' David shrugged philosophically. 'I had the same problem when—when Cathy died six months ago.' He shook his head. 'If it's news, they'll print it; good or bad.'

'This is definitely bad,' Molly said heavily. 'Especially now, when Crys and Sam are already so distracted over Peter.' She frowned. 'I think perhaps you had better lose that newspaper, Gideon,' she advised worriedly. 'Tell Crys, if she asks, that we weren't able to find one.'

'Don't worry, I intend to,' he assured her grimly. 'I also intend finding out who gave them this story in the first place.' He threw the newspaper down on the table in disgust.

'Who gave it to them…?' Molly repeated frowningly. 'You think someone actually told them about the christening?'

'Well, of course someone told them,' he rasped disgustedly. 'And after years of Sam keeping his whereabouts a secret, that damned newspaper has also stated if not the actual address then the exact location of this house.'

Molly could only stare at him, her cheeks white with dismay. After his experience with his ex-fiancée, Sam had good reason to value his privacy. Even more so since he had married Crys and they had baby Peter. As Molly had already said, this newspaper article could only be bad news.

'But who would do such a thing?' She shook her head dazedly.

'Yes—who *would* do such a thing?' Gideon grated coldly.

Molly looked up sharply, finding herself caught in the sudden glitter of that dark blue gaze.

He didn't think—? Surely he didn't believe that she had had anything to do with this outrage?

'The new *Bailey* series, and the people starring in it, is mentioned several times in the accompanying article,' Gideon bit out tersely.

Accusingly…?

But she would never… Could never…

Gideon could have no idea of the disruption that had

occurred in her own and their parents' lives twelve years ago, because of the vindictiveness of Sam's ex-fiancée. The constant hounding by the press, her parents actually having to move house, Molly having to change schools in an attempt to shield her from all the adverse publicity. The new school was where she had met Crys and the two of them had become such good friends...

But that was Gideon's real problem, wasn't it? Crys... Molly was very fond of Crys herself, but Gideon seemed to care only about her, about protecting her...

'I think I will come for that drive with you after all, David,' she told him woodenly, deliberately keeping her gaze averted from Gideon. She sensed he was still looking at her. But she had to get out of here, or this time she really would have to hit him!

'Great.' David grinned his satisfaction with the arrangement. 'And I shouldn't worry too much about that newspaper, Gideon,' he advised ruefully. 'It's Christmas; by the time the holidays are over everyone will have forgotten all about it.'

Molly wasn't so sure about that, and she could see by the continued grimness of his expression that Gideon wasn't convinced, either. But with it being Christmas Day tomorrow there really was nothing they could do about it now. And Gideon throwing out wild accusations—completely erroneous ones—certainly wasn't going to help the situation! But, by the same token, neither was her reacting angrily to them...

Which was why it was better if Molly removed herself from his company for the moment. Better for Gideon, that was. For herself, Molly would have liked to set him straight over several matters. For Crys and

Sam's sake she would keep her own counsel. For the moment...

'I certainly hope so.' Gideon nodded abruptly.

'Ready, Molly?' David prompted lightly.

She was more than ready to remove herself from the odious Gideon's company, not even bothering to say goodbye to him as she followed David out of the house.

Really, Gideon seemed to think she was to blame for everything that happened. Everything bad, that was.

But who could it have been who'd told the press about the christening? Because it certainly hadn't been her!

'Cheer up,' David advised lightly after they had driven in silence for several minutes. 'It may never happen!'

'It already has happened,' she returned gloomily. 'Surely you must realise Gideon thinks I told the press about the christening?'

'He doesn't think that really,' David assured her with a grin. 'He's only off with you because he likes you.'

'You have to be joking!' Molly spluttered.

'I didn't say he was happy about it,' David accepted slowly. 'But he does like you.' He nodded with certainty. 'And a little jealousy because you've come out with me this afternoon can't be a bad thing!'

Molly shook her head in disbelief. 'You're being as ridiculous as Crys now,' she dismissed disgustedly. 'I don't like Gideon.' Even less so now. 'And he doesn't like me. End of story,' she told David firmly.

'Sure,' he accepted unconvincingly.

'I mean it, David.' She gave him a warning glare. 'The sooner Christmas is over and I can get as far away from Gideon as it's possible to be, the better I shall like it.'

He gave her a brief narrow-eyed glance. 'Methinks the lady doth protest too much...'

'Will you just stop it?' Molly's hands were clenched tightly in her lap. 'The man is absolutely loathsome!' she stated determinedly, clearly remembering the accusation in his gaze earlier.

Except she couldn't quite deny—to herself, at least—her completely nerve-tingling awareness of Gideon.

But just because she was physically aware of him that didn't mean she had to like the man.

Of course it didn't.

Except now she *was* protesting too much. Damn it. And most of all damn Gideon Webber.

'I quite like him myself,' David said slowly. 'And he's obviously very fond of Crys.'

'Perhaps too fond,' Molly snapped before she had time to guard her words, and at once felt stricken at having spoken quite so bluntly.

She liked David, would be working very closely with him in future months, but that was no reason to have voiced her inner suspicions concerning Gideon's feelings towards Crys.

Her cheeks felt warm with embarrassed colour. 'What I meant to say was—'

'Forget it, Molly.' David reached over and briefly squeezed her arm. 'It's an interesting concept, I grant you that,' he added thoughtfully. 'But not one I should put too much credence in, if I were you,' he dismissed.

'No,' she accepted gratefully. She really would have to be more careful about making unguarded comments about Gideon. To anyone.

'I mean it, Molly.' David gave her a warm glance. 'Try thinking about it from Gideon's point of view—'

'Do I have to?' She grimaced.

He chuckled softly, shaking his head in gentle re-proof. 'From what I can gather, Crys is the only family Gideon has left. She *is* family, Molly,' he insisted softly as she looked sceptical. 'His parents both died years ago, and Crys was married to Gideon's younger brother. That brother is now dead, too. All Gideon has left of that relationship is Crys.' He shrugged. 'That's how I see it, anyway. I'm still extremely close to Cathy's parents,' he added huskily.

It was one way of looking at things, granted. But Molly wasn't convinced it was the right way as far as Gideon's feelings towards Crys were concerned...

Although it was definitely preferable to believing the man she was so attracted to was in love with another woman. Been there, done that.

'Before you start again, I did not tell any member of the press about the christening on Sunday,' Molly told Gideon defensively when she turned to find him stand-ing grim-faced behind her as she set about preparing their evening meal. Crys was still totally occupied up-stairs with the less-than-happy Peter.

His gaze narrowed. 'I—' He broke off as the tele-phone on the kitchen wall began to ring. 'Would you mind answering that?' he said slowly.

Molly looked from him down to her wet hands, where she was peeling potatoes, and then back at Gideon. 'It may have escaped your notice, but I'm a little busy at the moment!' she snapped irritably; in fact up to her arms in it was the description that readily came to mind.

Not that she at all minded preparing an evening meal in Crys's absence. In fact, she was more than pleased to have something to do. But at the same time she did not intend being harassed by Gideon. And the still-ringing telephone, like Gideon himself, was starting to grate on her nerves.

Gideon drew in a sharp breath. 'If I say please...?' he suggested tightly.

Molly blinked; that would certainly be a novelty. 'Well?' she pushed dryly when he made no effort to do so.

His eyes flared deeply blue. 'Please,' he finally bit out, through gritted teeth.

'Testy, testy,' Molly taunted as she moved to dry her hands before snatching up the receiver. 'Yes?' she prompted lightly.

Her query was met by silence. Not the silence of a call ended, but that slightly static silence that said the line was still open.

'Hello?' she said more strongly. 'Is there anyone there?' Her voice was sharp now. She was more and more convinced that there was someone on the end of the line. She could almost hear their breathing...

In answer to her last query there was a faint click on the line, the dialling tone immediately following.

Molly slowly put down the receiver before turning sharply to look at Gideon. 'What's going on?' she demanded to know.

'I have no idea.' He shrugged abruptly. 'But that's the third call like that since you left with David this afternoon. I wanted you to answer it this time to see if you got the same response I did when I answered the last two.'

'Hanging up?' Molly said slowly.

'Exactly,' Gideon confirmed grimly, thrusting his hands into his trouser pockets. 'Obviously the call wasn't meant for you, either,' he added frowningly.

Molly shook her head. 'Maybe it was just a wrong number?'

'Three times in as many hours?' Gideon said sceptically.

'It could be.' She shrugged dismissively, more interested in cooking dinner for them all than worrying about hang-up calls.

'Don't be ridiculous, Molly,' he snapped.

Her eyes widened indignantly. '*I'm* being ridiculous?' she repeated incredulously. 'Every time something bad happens around here you automatically assume I have to somehow be involved. No doubt you think I'm somehow responsible for these calls, too?' she challenged scathingly.

'Hardly, when you're standing right here beside me,' he returned harshly.

She shook her head disgustedly. 'I suppose that's one thing in my favour.'

Gideon drew in a harsh breath, obviously controlling his temper with effort. 'Look, I'm sorry if I was wrong earlier, concerning that article in the newspaper…'

'Are you?' Molly's eyes flashed disbelievingly. 'Are you really?' she repeated.

'Yes,' he hissed, his jaw tightly clenched, eyes darkly blue in his pale, strained face.

Molly frowned as a thought suddenly occurred to her. 'Do you think those calls could be from another reporter after a story? Or possibly even the same one?' she added hardly.

'They could be, I suppose,' Gideon said slowly. 'Although why would they keep hanging up in that way?'

Molly shrugged. 'Because it isn't Crys or Sam answering the calls?'

'But how would they know that?' Gideon didn't look convinced by this theory.

Neither was Molly, if the truth were known, but she couldn't think of any other explanation for them. Unless they really were just wrong numbers...

'I've disposed of the newspaper, by the way,' he added harshly.

'I never had any doubts that you would,' Molly returned with obvious sarcasm.

'Molly—'

'Gideon,' she interrupted firmly. 'It may have escaped your notice, but I'm trying to cook dinner for all of us.' She indicated the potatoes she had been peeling, and the duck sitting in the baking tray waiting to go in the Aga.

He frowned for several seconds, and then his attention shifted to the partly prepared food. Amusement glittered in those dark blue eyes when his gaze finally returned to hers. 'Do you actually know how to cook?' That amusement was reflected in his mocking tone.

Christmas is a time of 'peace and goodwill to all men', Molly, she reminded herself firmly. And one thing she had learnt about Gideon Webber these last few days—he was definitely a man.

She drew in a controlling breath. 'More than you do, I'm sure,' she told him with determined control; the duck would be much better cooked and then enjoyed by them all than aimed at this man's arrogant head.

'I'm sure, too,' he conceded with an acknowledging tilt of his head. 'The only thing I know about cooking is that one should keep the chef readily supplied with wine. Red or white?' he offered lightly.

Molly stared at him incredulously. Just when she

thought she really detested this man, he did something nice. Throwing her into complete confusion.

As if she wasn't confused enough already. She had every reason to loathe and detest this man, and yet every time he walked into a room she was physically totally aware of him.

Like now!

'Red, thanks,' she accepted stiltedly, before turning sharply away to bend down and put the duck in the oven. 'And, just to put your mind at rest about the cooking,' she told him, 'when I was ''resting'' about five years ago…' her tone was dry, as she knew that Gideon would be as aware as anyone else that the term 'resting', when applied to an actor, actually meant 'out of work' '…I helped Crys out in the kitchen of her restaurant. I'm sure it won't be up to her standard, but— Oh!' She had turned to find Gideon standing only inches away from her, and was suddenly breathless as she stared up into eyes the colour of a clear midnight sky.

'Oh, indeed,' Gideon murmured huskily, making no effort to give her the glass of wine he held in his hand.

Time seemed to stand still. The house was unusually quiet, with only the ticking of the kitchen clock on the wall beside them to tell them of the passing of time. Even Merlin was quiet as he dozed in front of the Aga.

Molly's mouth had gone dry, and colour warmed her cheeks as she saw Gideon's dark gaze follow the movement of her tongue across her lips.

She could barely breathe, was aware of Gideon with every sense and nerve of her body—aware of him in a way she had never been aware of any man before.

What would he say, this man who believed she had been his brother James's mistress, if the two of them were ever to make love and he discovered that she had never had a lover—that, at twenty-nine, she was still a virgin?

Well, that particular solution might be a little drastic—but at least he would know that his suspicions concerning herself and James were completely unfounded.

'Why are you smiling in that "I know something you don't" way?' Gideon prompted huskily, his dark gaze once again warily guarded.

It completely broke the moment of shared intimacy...

Thank goodness.

Molly sighed as she stepped thankfully away. 'I was merely wondering when you were going to give me my glass of wine,' she invented pointedly, at the same time drawing in deeply controlling breaths, completely flustered by these moments of intense intimacy she seemed to be sharing with Gideon more and more.

In the future—for the next three days, in fact—the less time she spent alone with Gideon, the better she would like it.

He looked down frowningly at the glass he still held, as if surprised to see it there in his hand. 'What can I do to help?' he offered abruptly, at the same time putting the glass of wine down on the worktop beside her.

Leave the kitchen and give her a few moments' respite from his totally evocative company seemed like a good idea to Molly right now.

Although, from the efficient way he picked up the vegetable knife and looked at her expectantly, she didn't think that suggestion was going to work. 'Finish the potatoes for me, if you will,' she dismissed airily, determinedly turning her own attention to preparing Brussels sprouts with almonds.

Molly wasn't under any illusions that the silence between them was in the least comfortable. She knew that just one word—the wrong word—could trigger hostilities between them once again.

Peace and goodwill—ha!

CHAPTER SEVEN

'WELL, isn't this a nice scene of domestic harmony?' David murmured approvingly a short time later.

Molly turned to give him a narrow-eyed warning look. Domesticity, my foot; Gideon was as domesticated as a feral cat. And, in view of the fact that they had been working together in tense silence for the last ten minutes or so, she doubted that he even knew what the word harmony meant as far as she was concerned.

'All you need is a pinafore, Gideon, and you'll completely look the part,' David added with teasing challenge, having given a hasty look round the kitchen to make sure they had put Merlin safely outside before coming completely into the room himself.

Gideon looked at the other man from under raised blond brows. 'And what part would that be, David?' he drawled softly.

The actor grinned unabashedly. 'Why, Assistant Chef, of course,' he said mockingly.

'Of course,' Gideon echoed derisively. 'Why don't you make yourself useful and pour us all some more wine?'

'I won't, if you don't mind.' David replenished their two glasses. 'Someone has to drive us all to church later tonight,' he reasoned. 'As you two seem to have done all the hard work towards dinner, it may as well be me.' He shrugged.

Molly had completely forgotten their plans to go to the late service that evening. 'Do you think Crys and

Sam will still want to go?' She frowned, having seen nothing of the other two since delivering Peter's medicine to them a couple of hours ago.

'Maybe not.' David grimaced. 'But that's no reason why we shouldn't.'

'Why you shouldn't what?' Crys asked as she came into the kitchen. 'Oh, thank you, Molly.' She hugged Molly when she saw that dinner was already well in hand. 'I feel awful for deserting you all like this today.'

'How is the little chap?' David was the one to ask gently.

'Much better, thank you.' Crys sighed her relief, looking less strained than she had earlier this afternoon. The colour was back in her cheeks, too. 'He's sleeping quietly at the moment, so Sam should be down in a minute or two. What were you talking about when I came in?' she prompted interestedly, smiling her thanks as she sat down and accepted the glass of red wine Gideon poured for her.

'Church later tonight,' David explained.

'Oh, yes—you must all go,' Crys insisted warmly. 'Sam and I went last year and it was very beautiful, with all the candles alight and decorated with holly. You—' She broke off as the telephone began to ring.

Molly froze at the sound, turning sharply to Gideon and finding her look returned frowningly as he, too, obviously wondered if this was yet another of those hang-up calls.

'I'll get it,' Sam told them as he came into the kitchen, and plucked the receiver from the wall. 'Yes? Speaking. Oh, fine thanks,' he answered warmly seconds later.

Much to Molly's relief, and Gideon's, too, if his

smile was anything to go by, this obviously wasn't another of those calls.

'Much better,' Sam continued. 'No, I'm sure there's no need for you to do that. Although…' He put his hand over the mouthpiece. 'Is there enough dinner for one extra?' he prompted softly.

'Molly?' Crys turned to her.

'I'm sure there is,' she confirmed lightly, wondering exactly who the 'one extra' was going to be; Sam's tone was extremely warm and cordial, so it certainly wasn't a reporter.

Sam removed his hand from the mouthpiece. 'Why don't you come over anyway and join us for dinner? No, of course you wouldn't be intruding,' he added firmly. 'We're eating about eight, so come about seven-thirtyish. I believe several of us are going to church later, if you would like to join us for that, too…? Fine, we'll see you later, then.' He rang off. 'Diana Chisholm is going to join us for dinner,' he announced happily.

'Oh, that's wonderful.' Crys smiled her pleasure. 'I didn't like the idea of her spending Christmas on her own.'

'You may as well open this house up for all waifs and strays!' David remarked caustically, scowling. Then he seemed to realise what he had just said. 'Sorry,' he muttered harshly. 'If you'll all excuse me?' He turned and strode purposefully from the kitchen.

'What's wrong with him?' Sam looked as dazed by the other man's abrupt departure as they had all been by the remark that had preceded it.

'My insensitivity, I think.' Crys gave a grimacing sigh. 'After all, it's David's first Christmas without Cathy, which can't be easy after all those years of marriage.' She stood up. 'I'll go and talk to him.'

'No, I'll go,' Gideon offered, putting down his wine-glass. 'It's a man thing,' he assured Crys gently as she would have protested. 'Less embarrassing all round if I go, and especially for David,' he added ruefully.

It might be less embarrassing for David, but Molly had serious doubts about Gideon being the one to deal with such a sensitive subject.

'Unless you would like to go?' Gideon paused beside Molly, obviously guessing at least some of her thoughts.

Although the mockery in his gaze seemed to imply he had completely misconstrued the reason for her ex-pression of doubt. As usual.

'Not at all,' she assured him lightly. 'As you say, it's a man thing.' She looked up at him challengingly.

She was not in the least interested in David in the way this man seemed to be implying she was, but if he wanted to go on thinking that, that was his problem.

Gideon continued to look at her for several long sec-onds, then with an abrupt nod of his head he followed the other man from the room.

'Phew,' Sam breathed ruefully. 'Exactly what's been going on here today while Crys and I have been oth-erwise occupied?' He looked questioningly at Molly.

Apart from Gideon insulting her at every opportunity, then almost kissing her, and a photograph of them all being spread all over the newspaper—giving yet another excuse for Gideon to be insulting to her—and then be-ing inundated with strange hang-up calls, absolutely nothing had been happening today!

All of which she had no intention of so much as mentioning to either Sam or Crys.

'Just normal Christmas Eve tensions,' she dismissed lightly. 'Now, tell me, Crys.' She turned to her friend and sister-in-law. 'Do you want me to serve an orange or an apple sauce with the duck this evening?'

Anything to do with cooking was guaranteed to distract Crys, and the two women discussed the merits of both sauces before deciding on apple. All the time Molly was aware of Sam watching her with amused green eyes, as if completely aware of her distracting tactics—and not fooled by them for a moment.

But then she and Sam had always been as close, if not closer, than real brother and sister. Sam was often able to tell what she was thinking before she was aware of it herself. She only hoped he didn't pick up on some of the things she had been thinking about Gideon Webber today. They were too contrary for her to make any sense of, let alone anyone else.

Think of the devil…

Molly felt herself stiffen defensively as Gideon strode back into the room, his good humour restored if his grin was anything to go by. Hopefully he had had the same success with David.

'Everything okay?' Crys prompted concernedly.

'He'll be down shortly,' Gideon reassured her. 'He's decided to shower and change before dinner.'

'Well, at least he is joining us.' Sam grimaced.

'Of course he is.' Gideon's grin widened. 'I only had to point out the advantages of having such a lovely and accomplished woman join us for dinner for him to agree to that.'

Oh, and what was she? Molly wondered disgruntledly. Chopped liver?

Probably, as far as Gideon was concerned, she accepted heavily.

Sam's actress sister—at the moment splattered with grease from basting the duck, her face flushed from the

Aga, her hair frizzed up from the heat—couldn't really compare to someone as coolly beautiful and caring as the doctor she had met earlier today.

Rather depressing, really, she acknowledged ruefully. Even if it was true.

'You two lovely ladies apart, of course,' Gideon added dryly. Rather too tardily, as far as Molly was concerned.

'Too late, I'm afraid, Gideon,' Crys told him laughingly, turning to link her arm with Molly's. 'Let's all have a bit of fun and dress up for dinner. After all, it is Christmas. Molly, what say you and I leave these two men to lay the table while we go upstairs and change before dinner?'

'Sounds good to me!' Molly grinned conspiratorially, deliberately putting her nose in the air as the two of them swept out of the room.

Crys gave a rueful shake of her head as they climbed the wide staircase together. 'So tell me, what's really been happening today while Sam and I have been upstairs with Peter?' she prompted dryly.

'Not a lot,' Molly said lightly, deliberately keeping her expression deadpan.

'Liar!' Her friend laughed softly. 'You and Gideon seem to be getting along together?'

'If by that you mean I haven't actually hit him over the head with one of your saucepans yet, then, yes, I suppose that we are,' Molly answered disgustedly.

Crys's chuckle deepened. 'Gideon is a love.'

Molly almost stumbled up the last stair in surprise at this statement. A love? Gideon?

'Well, I think he is,' Crys added with a frown of consternation at Molly's reaction to this statement.

'Probably because he is, as far as you're concerned,'

she dismissed. 'I'm a completely different matter, I'm afraid. Perhaps it's just that he doesn't approve of actresses,' she added, as Crys looked less than happy.

'But he did come and dispose of that spider for you last night,' Crys reminded her cajolingly.

'Crys, it's a mistake for you to try to matchmake between Gideon and me.' Molly didn't even attempt to correct her friend concerning Gideon's 'disposal' of the spider. What was the point? Probably she and Gideon would never meet again after this Christmas holiday. There was no point in upsetting Crys's friendship with Gideon just because she found him a sadistic swine.

'Sam's been talking to you,' Crys guessed indignantly.

'Not at all,' Molly said easily, having no intention of implicating Sam in any of this. 'I would have to be blind not to see what you're up to,' she told her friend affectionately. 'But just stop, hmm? I'm not Gideon's type. And he certainly isn't mine,' she added more forcefully. 'I've never been attracted to that arrogant, macho type.'

'But—'

'Excuse me, ladies,' cut in an icy-cold voice from behind them. 'But you appear to be blocking the stairway,' Gideon added pointedly as he stood on the step behind them.

Molly closed her eyes briefly before looking up at the ceiling above them, all other thoughts fleeing as she saw the yellow rose painted in the dome above. James's trade mark...

She became completely still. She had forgotten that she had recommended James's work to Sam when he'd been looking for an interior designer to come here four years ago, but that yellow rose above them in the domed ceiling reminded her all too forcefully of the friend, husband and brother the three of them had all lost.

For a few seconds everything seemed to stop, including time and sound, and a mellow calm settled over her before she once again became aware of exactly where she was. And whom she was with.

She turned sharply, hoping that Crys hadn't seen her brief distraction, or the reason for it; the last thing she wanted to do at this time was to remind Crys of the husband she had loved and lost. But she needn't have worried; Crys had been distracted herself by one of the Christmas decorations on the stair banister that had come loose, and she was attempting to fix it back in place.

Not so Gideon, Molly saw with dismay. His jaw was set rigidly, blue eyes glittering with fury as he glanced up at the domed ceiling and then back at her.

Molly stepped away. 'I'll see you both later,' she managed to murmur before hurrying up another set of stairs to her bedroom on the third floor.

She closed the door thankfully behind her, knowing it was pointless even trying to explain to Gideon what had happened just now; he didn't seem to believe a word she said anyway. And especially when it came to the subject of his brother James...

She was almost knocked off her feet as the door was pushed open behind her, and regained her balance to turn and see Gideon silhouetted in the doorway.

'What the hell do you think you're doing?' he snapped furiously, moving into the room to close the door behind him with barely suppressed violence, his eyes glittering dangerously as he looked across at her with unconcealed contempt.

Molly swallowed hard. She could try pretending she

had no idea what he was talking about, but she had a feeling that would just make him angrier still. If that were possible! But at the same time she knew he wasn't going to believe her if she told him the truth—that just for a moment, for a very brief moment, she had felt a closeness with James, an emotional affinity, and had mentally assured him that Crys was happy again now, that Sam would take care of her always.

If she even tried to put that into words she knew how stupid it would sound.

And to someone like Gideon, who seemed to enjoy thinking the worst of her, it would sound so much worse than stupid...

'Well?' he bit out harshly, a nerve pulsing in his jaw, hands clenched at his sides.

Molly drew in a deep breath. What could she say? How could she explain?

'How dare you moon about like some lovesick idiot?' Gideon rasped before she could formulate any sort of reply. 'James is dead,' he snapped viciously, before stepping forward to grasp her arms painfully in his hands and shake her slightly. 'Dead—don't you understand? When are you all going to accept that!'

Molly felt the colour drain from her cheeks at the stark brutality of his words. She knew James was dead, they all did, but that was no reason not to think of him sometimes. Especially now. Christmas was like that—a time of warmth and joy, but also a time to think of loved ones who were no longer here.

She shook her head. 'I have accepted it—'

'No,' he rasped forcefully, shaking her again. 'I don't think you have.'

Molly's breath caught sharply in her throat. 'I don't give a damn what you think—'

'In that case…' Without any warning, any indication of what was coming, Gideon's mouth came crashing down on hers.

Molly was too stunned by the assault to respond at first, her breath lodged somewhere in her chest as Gideon crushed her against the hardness of his body, his arms like steel bands, his mouth ruthlessly plundering her own.

But that blinding numbness only lasted for a matter of seconds, and then Molly started fighting against him in earnest, her hands pushing at his chest as she wrenched her mouth away from the punishing determination of his.

'Stop it!' she gasped, glaring up at him with pained brown eyes. 'Gideon, stop this!' she cried again as his eyes glittered fiercely down at her.

He became very still, his face pale, set in grim lines as he stared down at her with narrowed eyes, his hands still tightly gripping her arms.

Probably as well; she wasn't sure she wouldn't collapse completely if Gideon weren't holding her upright.

'Please—stop,' she groaned emotionally.

She simply couldn't take any more today. The last twenty-four hours seemed more like a hundred. And it wasn't over yet.

'It's Christmas,' she added huskily.

Gideon blinked, still frowning darkly, although the glitter seemed to be fading from his eyes.

He shook his head. 'What the hell am I doing?' he finally muttered self-disgustedly, releasing her abruptly to step away.

Molly swallowed hard. 'I have no idea. But I have a feeling you're going to regret having done it once you have time to think about it,' she added shakily.

One thing she was absolutely sure of was that the last thing Gideon really wanted to do was kiss her—at the time it had probably just seemed preferable to any other method of silencing her.

Gideon continued to stare at her for several long, breath-stopping moments, and Molly wasn't sure quite what he was going to do next. In the circumstances, he probably wasn't too sure himself.

He gave another shake of his head, frowning darkly now. 'I apologise for...for whatever that was,' he bit out abruptly, turning sharply away, seeming dazed by his own actions.

Molly felt her heart sink as she watched him walk heavily across the room. 'Gideon...!' she cried out as he opened the bedroom door.

'Yes?' He turned back to her, his expression bleak.

She bit her bottom lip, not quite sure what to say to him now that she had his attention, only aware that she couldn't let him leave like this, with so many things left unsaid between them. 'About James. I—we all still miss him,' she breathed huskily.

If anything he looked even bleaker. 'Some of us more than others, it would seem,' he rasped, not waiting for her answer, but letting himself quietly out of the room.

Molly sat down heavily on the bed to bury her face in her hands as tears fell hotly down her cheeks.

CHAPTER EIGHT

'YOU look gorgeous!' David told her admiringly as she entered the sitting-room a short time later to join the others for a pre-dinner drink. 'Like Mrs Christmas, in fact,' he added teasingly, obviously having got over his upset of earlier.

Or else he was just hiding it well...

Molly understood what he meant about the knee-length, figure-hugging Chinese-style red dress she was wearing this evening; it was a bright poppy-red that someone was sure to say didn't go with her copper-red hair.

Although Gideon seemed unusually quiet this evening, standing broodingly beside the fireplace, looking elegantly attractive in his black dinner suit and snowy white shirt. And as remote and cold as a statue as his gaze briefly met hers.

Molly quickly averted her own gaze, turning to smile at Sam as he handed her a glass of champagne. 'What are we celebrating?' she teased.

'The slightly late start of Christmas,' he returned ruefully. 'Diana is upstairs with Crys right now, checking on Peter, but she assured us that Peter really doesn't have chickenpox, and that he is much better already,' he added with satisfaction.

'That's wonderful,' Molly said with relief. 'Definitely worth drinking to.' She took a sip of the bubbly wine, without looking at Gideon this time to see if he was watching her. She had a feeling that looking at Gideon was going to be quite hard to do after that earlier scene in her bedroom.

'Where's Merlin?' she prompted, with nothing better to say.

Sam arched a mocking brow. 'Where do you think?'

She smiled. 'Upstairs, keeping watch over Peter.'

'Right first time!' Sam grinned. 'I—' He broke off as they heard the telephone ring in the kitchen. 'Now, who could that be—telephoning on Christmas Eve?' He frowned.

'I'll go; it could be the parents,' Molly told him quickly, putting down her wineglass to hurry across the room, not wanting anything to spoil this time for Sam and Crys now that the worry over Peter was apparently at an end. Something she couldn't guarantee if it should be another one of those hang-up calls.

'I'll answer it,' Gideon told her gruffly, and the two of them reached the sitting-room door at the same time.

Molly felt the colour warm her cheeks, not quite able to meet that piercing blue gaze as she looked up at him, 'Fine,' she accepted huskily, turning quickly away so that he shouldn't see how even being near him like this affected her after what had happened between them earlier.

Because, despite Gideon's anger, his forcefulness, Molly knew that part of her had wanted to respond to his kisses, that she had wanted to kiss away his anger, to know the deeply sensual man she sensed below that surface of fury.

Ridiculous when everything Gideon said, everything he did, told her of his contempt for her. He—

'Penny for them…?' David prompted as he moved to stand beside her, putting her glass of champagne back in her hand.

She gave a sad shake of her head. 'I can't make any sense of them, so why should you?'

David gave a rueful shrug. 'We're a strange collection of people, aren't we?' he murmured ruefully as Diana Chisholm and Crys entered the sitting-room. Both women smiled at Sam as he turned to them enquiringly. 'There's Crys and Sam, obviously the centre of this motley crew—'

'Speak for yourself,' Molly cut in teasingly.

He gave a nod of acknowledgement. 'And there's baby Peter, too, of course. Then there's Dr Chisholm: beautiful, probably only in her thirties, but obviously dedicated to her career. Then there's you: Sam's sister, Crys's friend, the only one of us who's really entitled to share this family Christmas. And there's me, of course, recently widowed, fighting shy of being anywhere that's going to remind me of Cathy and the Christmases we spent together.' He smiled self-derisively.

'Don't.' She put a sympathetic hand on his arm. 'Don't do this to yourself, David,' she urged. Though at the same time she was curious as to what his explanation would be for Gideon's presence here...

But as Crys brought Diana Chisholm over to formally introduce her to the two of them Molly knew she wasn't going to hear David's opinion of Gideon being there. Pity. That might have been worth hearing.

Where *was* Gideon? It had been some time since he went to answer the telephone call, so what was keeping him?

'Excuse me,' she murmured before slipping away, confident she could leave the slightly melancholy David in Crys's more than capable hands.

She found Gideon in the kitchen, standing in front of

the window, staring out, supposedly, up at the starlit sky. She came to a halt in the doorway, not sure whether or not she should intrude on what was obviously a moment of privacy. She decided not.

'Makes you realise how insignificant we all are, doesn't it?' Gideon murmured just as she would have turned and walked quietly away. He turned to face her, his face partly in shadow. 'The stars,' he explained at her puzzled look. 'Did you know that some of them have died, completely disappeared, before their glow is even apparent to the human eye? Quite—'

'Have you and David both forgotten to take your happy pills this evening?' Molly cut in pragmatically. 'You're both so introspective I think you must have done!' she explained as his eyes widened. Inwardly, she wondered how he had known she was standing in the doorway, sure that her high-heeled shoes hadn't made any noise as she walked down the thickly carpeted hallway. Eyes in the back of his head, probably; he certainly didn't seem to miss much.

Gideon continued to look at her for several seconds, and then his mouth began to twitch, his eyes to glow with suppressed laughter. 'If it happens again we can always rely on you to bring us back down to earth, can't we?' He was openly chuckling now.

She shrugged dismissively, not sure it was actually a compliment, but deciding to accept it as such. 'Who was on the telephone just now?' she prompted lightly; at least they weren't arguing for once.

'My assistant.' He grimaced. 'A client wants me to fly to Vienna the day after Christmas.'

'"All work and no play",' Molly quoted dismissively, suddenly wondering if his assistant was female, and also if their relationship was just business orientated. Surely it was a little unusual for an assistant to track you down at someone else's house on Christmas Eve, of all days, just to tell you about a commission?

Just as quickly she admonished herself for even thinking such a thing. What difference could it possibly make to her whether or not Gideon's relationship with his assistant was purely business—or his relationship with any other woman, for that matter?

'Not this time.' Gideon shook his head firmly. 'I'm fully booked until at least Easter; this client will just have to take a number.'

James, she knew, had been an extremely popular interior designer, but the name Gideon Webber had been in vogue long before James had come on the scene. Obviously his designs were still sought after.

'Come on,' Gideon said firmly, crossing the room in three strides. 'Let's go and join the others.' He took a firm hold of her elbow. 'And David was right, by the way,' he murmured as they approached the sitting-room. 'You do look gorgeous in that dress,' he enlarged at her questioning look.

Molly was so stunned at the unexpectedness of the compliment that she stopped dead in the hallway, looking up at him with widely surprised eyes.

She had taken great care with her appearance after a glance in the wardrobe mirror in her bedroom had confirmed her earlier suspicions that she looked a mess. She had showered and washed and styled her hair so that it fell in soft russet waves past her shoulders. Her make-up was golden, with the merest hint of green shadow on her lids, the lipgloss a perfect match in shade for the dress.

But the last thing she had expected was that Gideon would be complimentary about her appearance.

He was looking at her quizzically now, and Molly spoke quickly to bridge the awkwardness. 'You're looking pretty good yourself,' she said bluntly, at once cringing inwardly at her less-than-sophisticated answer.

He gave another grin, suddenly looking roguish. 'Well, at least you and I have taken our polite pills this evening,' he murmured dryly, before his expression darkened. 'Molly, I'm afraid things got rather out of hand earlier, and—'

'Please,' she cut in abruptly, no longer able to meet his gaze. 'Let's just forget about it.'

His head tilted towards her, his face only inches away from her own now, his hand beneath her chin so that she had no choice but to look at him. 'Can we do that?' he prompted huskily.

Well, she certainly couldn't—not when a part of her still burned to know where those kisses might have led if she hadn't stopped them so abruptly.

'Of course we can,' she assured him brittlely. 'It's Christmas,' she announced, with the same determination she had earlier. 'And we should all try to be nice to each other at Christmas.'

His mouth twisted derisively. 'I admire your sentiments—even if I think them somewhat ambitious.'

Especially where the two of them were concerned...

'Yes. Well.' She gave a rueful shrug. '"Go for it" has always been my motto. Now, I suggest we do join the others,' she added briskly, stepping away from him, her chin tingling from his touch. 'Before our polite pills wear off.'

To her surprise Gideon laughed out loud this time. Looking so attractive when he did so that Molly's breath caught in her throat.

'You know...' he sobered slightly, shaking his head

'...you aren't quite what I thought you were going to be.' This last came out in a slightly puzzled voice, as if he was surprised at the admission.

'I'm not?' Molly said warily.

He grimaced. 'No.'

She shrugged. 'Actually, I don't think I'm what you thought I was at all. But that's just my personal opinion, you understand?' she added dryly.

Gideon looked at her frowningly for several long seconds before once more taking a firm hold of her arm and opening the sitting-room door. 'Let's, as we've both already suggested, join the others,' he said grimly.

Molly wasn't sure what the state of play was between herself and Gideon after this latest exchange, but at least it helped to make the Christmas Eve dinner more enjoyable for all of them. The two of them were no longer snapping at each other, and even David seemed to have shaken off his mood of despondency as he conversed with Diana Chisholm about her work.

In fact, the dinner passed off quite enjoyably, with everyone complimenting her on her cooking. Molly was pleased by their compliments, while at the same time assuring them that Crys would have done a better job of it.

Even Peter joined them for a while when they reached the cheese and port stage of the meal, seeming much happier now, despite the sprinkling of spots on his delicate baby skin.

It certainly wasn't the time for the telephone to ring intrusively for the sixth time today.

'I'll go this time,' Molly said determinedly, even as she stood up, having already sensed Gideon's sudden tension as he sat beside her at the table. 'At this time of night it's sure to be a wrong number,' she added, after a dismissive glance at her wristwatch.

'I'll come with you,' Gideon put in abruptly, also standing up.

'There's no need,' Molly assured him with a warning glare; someone was going to suspect something if the two of them kept jumping up like this every time the telephone rang.

Especially as she wasn't really sure herself that there was any need for them to do so...

'I need to make a call myself,' he insisted firmly, following her from the room.

Molly turned to glare at him as she hurried to the kitchen to answer the telephone. 'You do realise that everyone is going to start speculating about the way we keep disappearing off together like this,' she snapped impatiently.

'Let them,' he came back harshly, lifting the receiver from the wall before Molly could even reach for it. 'Hello? No, this isn't Sam,' he answered slowly, giving Molly a raised eyebrow at actually receiving a response this time. 'Would you like me to—? Damn it,' he rasped, holding the receiver away from his ear before slamming it back on the wall. 'She rang off,' he muttered impatiently.

'She?' Molly prompted frowningly.

'She.' Gideon nodded grimly.

Molly eyed him warily. 'Why are you looking at me like that?' she asked slowly, very much afraid that the temporary truce between them was about to come to an end.

'Because Sam isn't here for me to look at *him* like that,' Gideon snapped, moving abruptly away from her to start pacing up and down the kitchen.

Molly watched him for several seconds, not at all sure she knew what was going on—she certainly had no idea what Gideon was thinking behind that grimly set mask.

She frowned. 'Gideon—'

'What does your brother think he's playing at?' Gideon bit out angrily, his eyes glittering deeply blue. 'Isn't a beautiful wife like Crys and a newborn son enough for him?'

'Well, of course it's… Gideon, what are you implying?' Molly stiffened indignantly as she began to get an inkling of exactly what Gideon was saying.

He continued his pacing. 'It's the usual scenario, isn't it? The mistress telephoning her lover over Christmas because he's spending time with his family and she feels left out—'

'Now, hold on just a minute,' Molly exploded incredulously. He couldn't really think that Sam…?

'Do you have another explanation for the way this woman keeps ringing off when it obviously isn't Sam answering her calls?' Gideon paused in his pacing to challenge her scathingly.

She glared at him. 'I don't have any sort of explanation for the telephone calls, or any reason for a woman to keep hanging up like that. But the one thing I do know is that Sam does not have a mistress.' She shook her head disgustedly. 'Having seen how happy he and Crys are, I don't know how you can even suggest such at thing. Unless you're just looking for an excuse to cause trouble between them because of the way you feel about Crys,' she added accusingly, her cheeks flushed with anger, her eyes glittering deeply brown.

Gideon became very still, every muscle and sinew of his body stiff with resentment. 'And exactly what do you mean by that remark?' His voice was dangerously quiet.

Molly raised her chin defiantly. 'Anyone with eyes in their head can see that you're in love with Crys yourself,' she felt stung into accusing.

And then she wondered at her temerity. Had she really just voiced what had until this moment been only suspicions?

Yes, she had! But in her own defence it had only been because of the things he was saying about Sam.

How dare he say those things about Sam?

After Sam's bad experience with his unbalanced ex-fiancée twelve years ago, he hadn't so much as looked at another woman until he'd met Crys. And, okay, it hadn't exactly been love at first sight between the two of them, she remembered with affection, but it was obvious to anyone that the two of them now loved each other very much, that neither of them had eyes for anyone else.

To anyone except Gideon, it would appear...

From the dangerous glitter in his eyes at the moment, she had a feeling that the only emotion he was feeling right now was murderous anger—towards her.

CHAPTER NINE

MOLLY eyed Gideon warily, unsure what was going to happen next—those 'polite pills' had most definitely worn off.

'How dare you say something like that to me?' Gideon demanded coldly.

'How dare you say something like that about Sam to me?' she returned heatedly, her hands clenched at her sides as she met his gaze unflinchingly.

He gave an impatient shake of his head. 'Forget about that for the moment. Let's concentrate on—'

'No. Let's not forget about it!' Molly cut in determinedly. 'Your accusations…your suspicions about Sam and some other woman are totally unfounded,' she insisted firmly. 'Just something nasty and trumped-up because—'

'I would advise you not to repeat what you just said about my feelings towards Crys,' Gideon put in softly, a nerve pulsing in his tightly clenched jaw.

Molly faced him unblinkingly. 'Why not?' she scorned. 'Because, no matter what accusations you may make about other people, you are above such things? Or because it strikes a little too close to home? What—? Oh!' She had time only to gasp before his mouth took fierce possession of hers.

And yet somehow it wasn't a kiss of anger as before…

Gideon held her captive merely with his lips, plundering hers, and a light cupping of a hand on each of her cheeks. He held her face up to his, the kiss gentling after that first assault, sipping and tasting.

Heat coursed through her as she responded to those kisses, an aching need engulfing her. Her body curved into the hard length of his as if by instinct, and every hard contour told of his own rising desire.

His lips left hers to travel down the scented column of her throat, and the heat of his breath, the moist warmth of his lips against her skin ignited a fire wherever they touched.

She wanted this man.

Oh, how she wanted him!

His tongue probed the hollows at the base of her throat, dipping and tasting, and Molly shook with desire as she clung mindlessly to the width of his shoulders, the heat of his body matching hers.

She gasped as his teeth bit the lobe of her ear, the gasp turning to a throaty groan as that bite turned to a sensuous nibbling that raised her temperature even higher.

Finally those lips returned to hers, easily transmitting Gideon's passion and desire, and Molly returned those emotions as she pressed closer against him.

'Hmm-hmm,' interrupted a softly teasing voice. 'When you have quite finished seducing my little sister, Gideon...' Sam drawled as the two of them sprang abruptly apart, 'Diana has received a call on her mobile and won't be able to join us in going to church, after all; I thought the two of you might want to come and say your goodbyes,' he told them pointedly.

For a few moments Molly had trouble remembering who Diana was, and from the frown on Gideon's face he wasn't faring much better.

Although he recovered more quickly than she did,

straightening purposefully before nodding abruptly. 'I'll go through now,' he bit out tersely, giving a brief, dismissive nod that included both Molly and Sam before striding from the room.

Molly let out a shaky breath, momentarily closing her eyes, sure she must have imagined what had passed between herself and Gideon just now. Because it hadn't been anger. And it hadn't been disgust. To her, at least, it had felt like something else entirely.

She needed time to think, time to analyse what she thought had happened—

Sam was eyeing her mockingly when she opened her eyes, his smile one of teasing affection. 'Anything I should know about, little sister?' he asked softly.

Not until she had worked out for herself what just now had been all about. If she ever did.

And Sam certainly didn't need to know that one of his guests believed he was having an affair with another woman, Molly recalled frowningly, the rosy haze that had briefly surrounded her disappearing completely at this recollection.

No matter how it might have felt to her at the time, Gideon had kissed her initially because of the accusations she had made concerning his own feelings towards Crys. And she mustn't forget that fact.

'Not a thing,' she assured Sam lightly, moving forward to link her arm with his. 'Let's go and say good night to Diana.'

'Fine with me.' Her stepbrother nodded. 'But don't think you can avoid answering me forever,' he warned teasingly. 'Something is definitely going on between you and Gideon,' he stated with certainty.

'Something' definitely was—she just had no idea what.

*   *   *

Neither did she have any clearer an idea once she was alone in the house with only Peter a couple of hours later, having insisted on being the one who stayed behind with the baby while the others all went to the late church service.

'You're my idea of the ideal male companion,' she told the baby ruefully as he slept in the cot in his nursery. 'Totally uncomplicated.' She smiled. 'You cry when you're hungry, and sleep when you aren't.'

Peter gave a brief smile in his sleep, as if in sympathy with her, although Crys had assured Molly that those smiles were of the windy type.

'What am I going to do, hmm?' she mused as she stood up and moved to the window, staring out at the starlit sky much as Gideon had done earlier this evening in the kitchen.

Gideon.

Every thought, everything she said, all seemed to come back to Gideon just recently. Which wasn't surprising, considering the circumstances, but she could do with a little respite now and again. Like ten years or so.

'He kisses me, Peter,' she continued slowly, 'and yet I'm not even sure that he likes me. If you had asked me yesterday I would have been absolutely sure that he didn't!' She grimaced.

Earlier today she had been sure of the same thing. And yet this evening...

There had been none of his earlier contempt in the way he had kissed her this evening, none of the anger, either. Just... Just what?

She really didn't know.

She did know that she was becoming far too attracted to him. Possibly more than attracted.

What did that mean?

She couldn't be falling in love with Gideon! Could she…?

Molly gave a pained groan as she realised that she already had, that every word Gideon said, every gesture he made, affected her more deeply than any other man she had known.

Great!

Another Molly blunder. She had fallen in love with the one man guaranteed to hate her.

She—

She frowned slightly as she saw car headlights at the top of the driveway, and glanced down at her watch. The others couldn't be coming back from church yet; it was only just after midnight, and the service hadn't started until eleven-thirty.

But there were no other houses down this stretch of road, so the car had to be coming here. Unless it was some late-night revellers who had lost their way?

Even as she thought this she saw the car turn in the driveway and disappear back down the road.

'Too much Christmas spirit,' she told Peter, though the baby was sleeping on unconcernedly, she discovered as she glanced back into his cot. Great; she was talking to herself now.

She had never realised how creepy it was being alone here late at night. She had always had Sam here in the past, and latterly Crys and Sam. But it definitely wasn't a place she would want to spend too much time in alone. She wondered how Sam had stood it all those years before he and Crys were married.

'I know he had you.' She grimaced apologetically at Merlin as he lifted his huge head to look at her, almost as if he had guessed her thoughts. 'But it's still a little creepy. Come on,' she prompted the dog, deciding it was probably best if she kept herself busy. 'Let's go down and prepare mulled wine and mince pies for the returning carollers.'

Nevertheless, she pulled down all the blinds at the kitchen windows before preparing the wine and putting the mince pies in the warming oven. 'Just in case,' she told Merlin ruefully.

To say she was more than a little relieved when she heard the crunch of gravel outside to announce the return of Gideon's Jaguar—the car the others had elected to go to church in—would be putting it mildly. Every creak of a tree branch outside, the rustle of fallen leaves on the driveway, even the whoosh of the central heating as it went into action, had seemed intensified in the stillness of the house, making her slightly jumpy.

'Oh, wonderful!' Crys enthused as she came in the kitchen door first and smelt the wine and mince pies, her cheeks rosy from the chill night air, her eyes bright with happiness. 'Has Peter been okay?' she added anxiously.

'Of course,' Molly reassured her, smiling at Sam and David as they came into the kitchen, but quickly averting her gaze before Gideon entered, obviously having lingered to lock up the car. 'Go up and check on him if you want to,' she told Crys affectionately, turning to pour mulled wine for them all as her friend hurried off up the stairs to check on the baby.

But all the time Molly was aware of Gideon's brooding presence where he stood next to the Aga, warming his hands. Even more so now that she had realised she had stupidly fallen in love with the man. It made her other ill-fated love of over three years ago seem quite sane in comparison.

She took the plate from the warming oven. 'Mince pie, anyone?' she offered stiltedly, her gaze still lowered so that she didn't actually have to look at Gideon.

'Thanks.' David put down his mulled wine and helped himself to one. 'I don't know about the rest of you, but I intend going up to bed as soon as I've had these; I'm absolutely bushed.'

'So am I,' Molly agreed quickly, having no intention of lingering down here and possibly being drawn into a late-night conversation that would include Gideon.

'I'm just going to take Merlin out for a last stroll,' Sam told them. 'Crys spent hours making those mince pies, so you had better keep me one, Molly.' He grinned.

'Will do,' she assured him lightly. 'Mince pie, Gideon?' she offered abruptly, still not quite looking at him.

'Thanks,' he murmured huskily, his hand briefly coming into Molly's lowered line of vision.

It was a strong-looking hand, the fingers long and artistic, the nails kept short, his wrists wide, covered in soft blond hair, making Molly wonder if he had that same downy hair on the rest of his body. It was a thought guaranteed to make her completely lose her appetite—for mince pies, anyway.

'Aren't you having one?' Gideon prompted softly.

'Er—no.' Her mouth had gone so dry she would probably choke on what she knew was mouthwatering pastry. 'I had one earlier, while you were out,' she dismissed, turning away.

Her hand shook slightly as she took a much-needed sip of her mulled wine. She recognized that the situation between Gideon and herself was becoming intolerable if she could no longer even look at him.

'As it's after midnight—Happy Christmas, Molly.' David moved to kiss her on both cheeks. 'And many of them,' he told her warmly as he stepped back.

'You, too.' She smiled, her heart suddenly fluttering as she wondered if Gideon might decide to do the same; she wasn't sure how she would respond if he did.

But she was saved from answering that question by the kitchen door opening. Sam stood in the doorway, his expression one of impatient exasperation.

'Merlin has run off and isn't responding when I call him,' he bit out irritably. 'Would the two of you mind coming out and helping me look for him?' He looked at Gideon and David.

'I'll come,' Molly offered, having taken one look at David's face and realised he still wasn't too sure of the Irish Wolfhound's temperament. 'David is exhausted, and I could do with a walk in the fresh air anyway,' she added as she put down her glass and collected her coat and scarf from the back of the door.

'I owe you one,' David told her ruefully as she followed Sam and Gideon outside.

She paused to grin at him. 'Don't worry, I'm sure I'll be able to think of some way in which you can repay me.'

'Think away,' he invited. 'After all, I have to keep my leading lady happy, don't I?' he added teasingly.

Molly was still grinning as she closed the kitchen door behind her. Although her smile faded as she turned and found herself face to face with Gideon.

Hie mouth twisted derisively as he looked down at her. 'How touching.'

Molly opened her mouth to give a sharp reply to his obvious sarcasm. And then closed it again. What was the point? Gideon was never going to have a good opinion of her, so why bother to even try?

'We're supposed to be looking for Merlin,' she reminded him abruptly.

'Of course.' He gave a mocking inclination of his head, putting his hand out in a gesture for her to precede him.

Molly was glad to move away from the light given out by the kitchen window, knowing her cheeks were flushed, her eyes overbright—and not from the chill of the cold night air, either.

'Molly…?'

She froze at the sound of Gideon's voice, her shoulders tense as she slowly turned to face him, her expression wary. 'Yes?' she prompted reluctantly.

He was scowling darkly, drawing in a harsh breath before answering. 'Nothing.' He shook his head impatiently. 'Let's go and look for this silly dog.'

But ten minutes of shouting and looking proved completely unsuccessful. Merlin was nowhere in sight. Sam was looking worried rather than impatient when the three of them once again joined up outside the house.

'He's probably gone off chasing rabbits again,' Molly reassured lightly. 'You know how he loves to do that.'

'Maybe,' Sam answered slowly. 'I just—' He broke off as a whining and scrabbling noise suddenly became apparent to them all. 'What the—?' He strode determinedly round the side of the house, with Molly and Gideon following him just in time to see him open the door to the garden shed, and a relieved Merlin rushing out into the darkness to jump up at him ecstatically.

'Panic over,' Gideon drawled ruefully as they strolled over to join Sam and the happily barking dog.

'Shh, Merlin, you'll wake Peter up,' Sam murmured, still stroking the dog as he looked around distractedly.

'Everything okay?' Gideon prompted concernedly.

'Hmm.' Sam nodded, straightening. 'I'm just wondering how Merlin got shut in the shed in the first place, that's all.' He shrugged. 'Probably I just left it open earlier and it blew shut behind him,' he decided.

'He's safe now. That's the important thing,' Molly said encouragingly as she linked her arm with his. 'Let's all go in out of the cold, hmm?' She smiled reassuringly.

But her inner thoughts were less assured. Those strange telephone calls today—definitely not from any mistress of Sam's! The car headlights she had seen at the end of the driveway earlier—and now Merlin somehow getting himself shut in the garden shed.

It was that 'somehow' that bothered her.

Sam might have forgotten to shut the shed earlier. And Merlin might have wandered inside. And the wind might have blown the door shut behind him.

It just seemed to Molly that there were an awful lot of 'mights' in the scenario...

CHAPTER TEN

'WAITING up so that you can tell Father Christmas personally that you've been nice rather than naughty?' an all-too-familiar voice drawled mockingly as Molly sat alone in the kitchen two hours later, drinking a mug of coffee.

She had drawn in a sharp breath at the first sound of Gideon's voice, and released that breath in a heavy sigh as she registered the deliberate insult in his words. 'My mother always told me that if you can't say anything nice, don't say anything at all!' Molly snapped impatiently, leaning back in her chair to look at Gideon where he stood in the doorway.

Sam had settled Merlin down in the kitchen before going up to bed when they had all come in a couple of hours ago, and Molly and Gideon had followed him up the stairs to their own bedrooms. But, having undressed and gotten into bed, Molly had found herself unable to sleep. Finally she had given up the effort half an hour ago, in favour of pulling on a pair of denims and an old rugby top of Sam's to come downstairs and make herself a pot of coffee.

From the look of Gideon he had also gone to bed. He was no longer wearing his dinner suit, but a pair of faded blue denims and a dark blue tee shirt, his hair slightly tousled.

In fact, he looked altogether too approachably attractive for Molly's peace of mind.

He moved farther into the dimly lit room, the light

over the Aga their only illumination. 'Having now met Caroline, I appreciate what a graciously beautiful woman she is, and I stand corrected,' he drawled, pouring himself a mug of coffee from the pot and pulling out the chair opposite Molly's to sit down at the table.

Molly eyed him defensively. 'Hard to believe such a "graciously beautiful" woman could be my mother, isn't it?' she snapped disgustedly.

Gideon gave a humourless smile. 'I didn't say that.'

'You didn't have to,' Molly scorned. 'You—'

'Molly, I didn't come down here to argue with you,' he cut in quietly.

She eyed him warily for several long seconds, and Gideon steadily returned that gaze. 'Then why did you come down?' she finally prompted slowly.

He shrugged. 'For the same reason as you, I expect; because I couldn't sleep.'

Her mouth twisted derisively. 'Worried in case Father Christmas doesn't think you've been nice this year, either?'

He smiled as she neatly returned his jibe. 'There is that, I suppose,' he allowed. 'But, actually, no.' He sobered, frowning. 'Molly, what do you think is going on?'

She gave him a startled look. Was it so obvious that she was in a complete turmoil concerning her recently realised feelings for this man? If it was, then she—

'I'm talking about those telephone calls,' Gideon continued evenly.

Molly glared at him. 'I've already told you—they are not, as you suggested earlier, from any mistress of Sam's!'

He nodded. 'I'm beginning to agree with you.'

'Big of you!' she snapped scathingly.

Gideon gave a sigh. 'Molly, whatever the argument might be between the two of us, let's just forget it for a moment and concentrate on this other matter, hmm?'

Whatever the argument might be between the two of them...

It wasn't exactly an argument any more, was it? Gideon either insulted her or kissed her. And as for her own feelings...

'What other matter?' she prompted impatiently, wishing she had never come down here for a mug of coffee. The last thing that was going to help her get to sleep was another of these heated conversations with Gideon!

'The telephone calls—don't jump in again, Molly,' he said wearily. 'Just hear me out, hmm?' he suggested firmly. 'You have to admit those telephone calls are odd, to say the least.'

'Yes,' she allowed abruptly.

'Then Merlin disappeared and we found him shut in the garden shed,' Gideon murmured frowningly.

'Somehow,' Molly confirmed.

'Exactly.' Gideon nodded. 'What is it?' He eyed Molly searchingly as she chewed on her bottom lip. 'What else has happened?' he guessed shrewdly.

Was her face really that easy to read? If it was, in view of the way she had discovered she felt towards this man, she had better start guarding her expression a bit more!

She shrugged. 'It could just be nothing...'

Gideon sat forward tensely. 'What could?'

She grimaced, not sure that the two of them weren't just becoming paranoid. 'There was a car in the driveway earlier. When you were all at church. But whoever it was they didn't stay there—just turned around and drove away again,' she added quickly as Gideon's frown turned to a scowl. 'It could have been Diana Chisholm, I suppose,' she said suddenly, brightening slightly. 'Maybe she got her house-call over quite quickly and thought she could join us in going to church, after all, and then she saw how late it was and changed her mind?' She trailed off weakly as she realised she sounded as if she was grasping at straws.

'Maybe,' Gideon acknowledged slowly, not seeming to think she was grasping at straws at all. 'It might be worth calling her tomorrow and checking that out.'

Molly frowned when she saw how grim Gideon still looked. 'Gideon, what do *you* think is going on?'

'I have no idea,' he answered her honestly.

But the fact that he did think something was going on only reawakened Molly's earlier feelings of unease—just when she had been prepared to dismiss her fears as being late-night jitters and tiredness.

There was no denying that it hadn't only been thoughts of Gideon that had been keeping her from sleeping earlier.

Only thoughts of Gideon...

It was like saying it was only an iceberg—when you knew very well that ninety per cent of it was below the surface of the water, and—like Gideon—extremely dangerous to the unsuspecting.

But she had also been wondering if there was any connection between those telephone calls, the car she had seen earlier, and Merlin's disappearance. Why she had been wondering that, she had no idea, but if Gideon's thoughts and concerns were anything to go by she wasn't the only one with a vivid imagination.

'It's probably nothing, you know,' she told him ruefully.

'Probably,' he agreed unconvincingly.

Molly gave him a sharp look. 'I don't think you should mention any of this to Crys and Sam,' she warned softly.

He gave her a piercing look. 'I'm not completely stupid.'

She had never for a moment thought he was in the least stupid—many other things, but stupid certainly wasn't amongst them.

She gave a deep sigh, standing up to place her empty mug in the dishwasher. 'I think I'm ready to go back to bed.'

Gideon raised a dark blond brow. 'Is that an invitation?' he drawled mockingly.

It hadn't taken him long to return to being that derisive stranger.

Molly eyed him tauntingly. 'What do you think?'

He grimaced, smiling slightly. 'I think I would be pushing my luck to expect you to say anything but no. But you can't blame a man for trying!'

This man she could blame. Because once in this man's arms it would be easy to forget that he didn't like her, so good to forget that. But the repercussions certainly wouldn't be worth it.

'I suppose not,' she answered dryly, knowing she should leave, but slightly reluctant to do so. These few minutes' conversation, during the quiet early hours of the morning, had been something of a truce. Tomorrow, she didn't doubt, they would be back to their normal armed warfare.

Gideon eyed the rugby top she wore. 'Sam's?' he guessed dryly.

The top reached almost down to her knees, and the sleeves were pushed back so that the cuffs shouldn't hang off the ends of her hands. But it was comfortable, and at three-thirty in the morning that was what she wanted to be.

'I certainly hope so—otherwise I've lost an awful lot of weight!' she teased lightly.

'You're perfect just as you are,' Gideon said huskily.

Molly's breath caught in her throat, her eyes wide as she stared at him. Had Gideon, of all people, just given her a compliment?

No, he couldn't have done.

Could he…?

Gideon gave a slight smile as he saw the disbelief on her face that she was just too surprised to hide. 'I've given you rather a hard time over the last few days, haven't I?' he murmured huskily.

Molly eyed him warily. 'No harder than I've given you,' she answered guardedly, remembering his anger earlier this evening when she had mentioned his feelings towards Crys.

Feelings, she realised with a sudden jolt, that he had been angry about her mentioning but had never actually denied…

Gideon stood up abruptly. 'Don't start letting your imagination run away with you again,' he advised her harshly.

Molly's chin rose defensively. 'Isn't that what we've both been doing these last few minutes?' she challenged. 'There is probably no connection at all between those telephone calls, the car I saw and Merlin getting lost,' she said impatiently. 'Emotions just seem to run a little high at Christmas time.' She gave a derisive shake of her head.

'Is that what it is?' Gideon murmured softly, moving silently across the kitchen to stand only inches away from her. 'Is that the reason that at any given moment

I either want to smack your bottom or kiss you? And I'm never quite sure which it's going to be until the moment happens.' He shook his head. 'Does that mean that in two days' time this madness is going to stop?' he added hopefully.

Molly stared up at him, too much aware of the silence of the sleeping house and its inhabitants not to know how dangerous this particular situation was. Especially as she knew herself to be in love with this man.

But how did Gideon feel about her? Like smacking her or kissing her, he had claimed, with little to choose between the emotions.

'I expect it does.' She nodded abruptly.

'Pity,' Gideon bit out, holding her gaze locked with his.

Molly moistened dry lips, swallowing hard. Exactly what had he meant by that? He couldn't actually be *enjoying* this roller coaster of feelings every time the two of them were together?

'You're very kissable, you know, Molly,' he added huskily, his gaze sliding to the movement of her tongue across her lips.

He eyes widened in alarm at how quickly the atmosphere had changed between them. From antagonism to intimacy in a matter of seconds. And it was wrong. All wrong.

She eyed him with deliberate mockery. 'So I've been told,' she taunted.

His head came up, his mouth tight as his narrowed gaze clashed with hers. Clashed and held, in the mental battle of wills taking place between them.

To Molly's chagrin she was the first to look away, unable to sustain the challenge she had initiated between them because Gideon was standing close enough for her to be able to feel the heat of his body, to faintly smell the aftershave she knew he favoured.

'You did that on purpose,' he rasped suddenly, reaching out to grasp the tops of her arms.

Well, of course she had done it on purpose—how else could she have broken the intimacy that had been deepening between them by the second? Although she only seemed to have made the situation worse—Gideon was actually touching her now. And every time he did that her legs went weak at the knees.

'Why, Molly?' He shook her slightly. 'What are you running away from?'

'You, of course,' she gasped, staring up at him incredulously. 'It isn't very comfortable for me being on the receiving end of your wanting to either smack my bottom or kiss me.'

Gideon became very still, his eyes dark as he looked at her. 'At the moment I want to kiss you,' he murmured throatily.

'I know,' she groaned.

She had known that for the last few minutes—would be a fool not to know that. But where would that get them? Nowhere, she knew. Which was why it would be better for everyone if it didn't happen.

Except she wanted him to kiss her, too—ached to have him kiss her, to finish what they had started earlier!

'Molly…!' Gideon had time to murmur her name gruffly before his mouth once again claimed hers.

He was right. This was madness. But it was a madness Molly was no more able to stop than Gideon apparently was, and her lips parted to the pressure of his, her body curving against his hard contours even as her hands moved up over his shoulders, her fingers becoming entwined in the blond thickness of his hair.

These emotions had just been put on hold, she realised dazedly. Sam's interruption earlier had been only a respite from a desire neither of them seemed able to resist.

Gideon raised his head slightly to look at her. 'Why is it we're always in the kitchen when I kiss you?' he murmured self-derisively, his lips lightly grazing her temple.

'Because it's the warmest room in the house?' she suggested huskily, aware of this man with every fibre of her body.

Gideon looked at her with dark, fathomless eyes. 'I'm very warm. Aren't you?'

Warm? She was on fire!

'Quite warm,' she answered softly, suddenly shy. The time, the stillness of the house, was making it seem as if they were the only two people on the planet.

'Let's go into the sitting-room,' Gideon suggested gruffly, and he took her hand in his and turned to leave the kitchen.

Molly hesitated. The fire still glowed in the sitting-room. There was a sofa—a very comfortable one—in the sitting-room. And this was Gideon, a man who had expressed nothing but contempt for her.

She shook her head. 'Gideon, I don't think—'

'No—don't think,' he encouraged throatily, turning back to cup one side of her face with the warmth of his hand. 'Whenever the two of us start to think, collectively or singly, that's when things go wrong between us.' He bent his head to kiss her lingeringly on the lips. 'Don't think, Molly,' he urged persuasively.

She couldn't. Not when he kissed her with such aching passion. And she followed as he once again turned to leave the room.

She had been right about the sofa; it was comfortable. She sank back against the cushions as Gideon began to kiss her once again.

'You did look very beautiful tonight in that red dress,' he told her huskily as his lips travelled the length of her neck to the hollows of her throat. 'But all I wanted to do all evening was strip it from you!' he added achingly, before his lips returned to hers, fierce passion making any more talk between them impossible.

Molly's heart had leapt in her chest at Gideon's admission concerning her red dress, and her lips opened to his now as he deepened the kiss to intimacy.

His back was warm beneath his tee shirt, the muscles rippling beneath her fingertips as she touched him there, gasping slightly as his hands began to caress beneath her own top.

Only intending to come downstairs for a quick mug of coffee, she had merely pulled the rugby top and denims on over her nakedness, and Gideon groaned his approval as his searching hand encountered her bare breast.

It was Molly's turn to groan as Gideon cupped and caressed her nakedness, her nipple already pert and inviting as a thumbtip moved across it in a light caress.

And all the time his lips continued to possess hers, and Molly was aware only of him, of the touch of his mouth and hands on her lips and body.

Her hands clutched convulsively in the hair at his nape as he moved his lips to her naked breast, and she seemed to stop breathing altogether as he drew the sensitive tip into the moist warmth of his mouth, his tongue a rasping caress.

Molly was aware of every muscle and sinew of him as he lay half across her on the length of the sofa, his long legs entangled with her own, the hardness of his thighs telling of his own desire—if she had needed any telling.

'I want you, Molly,' he groaned as his mouth returned to hers and his hands now caressed the fiery tips of her breasts. 'God, how much I want you.'

She wanted him, too—too much to be able to say no to anything he asked of her.

His face was slightly flushed, his eyes glittering darkly as he raised his head to look at her, one of his hands moving to cup beneath her chin, his thumb running lightly over lips swollen from the hungry kisses they had just shared. 'Say you want me, too, Molly,' he encouraged huskily.

She didn't have to say it—knew it had to be obvious when her whole body was on fire. Even the blood in her veins seemed to flow more heatedly, making her aware of every pulsing inch of her body, from the soles of her feet to the top of her head.

'Say it, Molly!' he urged again. 'Tell me—' He broke off abruptly. 'What's that?' He frowned his confusion.

Molly frowned too as she became aware of a loud scrabbling noise somewhere in the house.

'A sleigh with eight reindeer on the roof, do you think?' Gideon suggested incredulously.

Molly gave a shaky smile. 'Somehow I doubt that very much,' she answered ruefully, very much aware of their closeness. Gideon's bared chest was against her own, covered in that downy blond hair, as she had imagined it was.

'So do I.' Gideon gave a dazed shake of his head as he raised himself slightly. 'What the—?' He gasped as the sound of loud barking suddenly broke the silence around them.

'It's Merlin,' Molly said concernedly, struggling to sit up.

'I realise that, but—hell, if we don't stop him he's going to wake the whole house up in a minute!' Gideon rasped, standing up to stride forcefully from the room with the obvious intention of silencing the dog.

Molly took a little longer to regain her equilibrium, still trembling with desire as she sat up to watch Gideon leave, her cheeks fiery red as she hastily pulled the rugby shirt down over her nakedness.

'Saved by the dog' didn't sound quite the same as the original quote, but it was no less the truth, for all that. If Merlin hadn't begun barking like this, shattering the intimacy between them, then she knew she would have told Gideon just how much she wanted him.

Too much!

CHAPTER ELEVEN

NOT that Gideon seemed to be doing too good a job of silencing Merlin. The sound of the dog's barking was interspersed with low growls, too, now, and the cacophony became louder as Molly hurried down the hallway to the kitchen.

Merlin was scrabbling at the back door when Molly entered the room, and Gideon was doing everything he could to calm him—from talking to him soothingly to raising his voice sharply, even going down on his haunches and trying to hold the dog and silence him that way.

This was something Merlin took great exception to, growling even deeper in his throat, baring his teeth in displeasure.

'He wants to go outside,' Molly advised him worriedly.

Gideon turned to scowl at her. 'I know what he wants, Molly,' he bit out frustratedly. 'I'm just not sure it's a good idea to let him out,' he added slowly.

She looked down at him frowningly. 'Why not?'

'Because… Just because.' He amended whatever he had originally been going to say, straightening to look down frustratedly as Merlin still scrabbled frantically at the door. 'I know this is a large house, but nevertheless I have no doubt that he's woken everyone in it by now—'

'He has indeed,' Sam muttered grimly as he came into the room. 'Silence, Merlin!' he instructed sharply.

Amazingly, the huge dog went quiet—although he still stood staring at the back door, panting heavily.

Sam, a white bathrobe pulled on over his nakedness, ran a hand through his already tousled hair. 'This is turning into one hell of a Christmas.' He shook his head dazedly.

'Isn't it?' Gideon agreed dryly.

Molly didn't look at him—couldn't look at him—but nevertheless she knew that last remark had been directed at her as much as at Sam.

It was turning into one hell of a Christmas for her, too. So much so that Molly had no idea where it was all going to end. But end it must. With or without this situation resolved between Gideon and herself.

'What's wrong with him?' Sam frowned as Merlin dropped to the floor, his nose pressed against the door as he once again began to rumble low in this throat.

Gideon straightened. 'Something outside disturbed him. A cat, possibly a fox.' He shrugged.

'I see,' Sam said slowly, seeming to look at the two of them for the first time and frowning thoughtfully as he took in their dressed appearance. 'And the two of you rushed down here to try to quieten him before he woke us all up?'

'Yes—'

'No,' Molly cut across Gideon's deliberate evasion, feeling the warmth in her cheeks as he looked at her frowningly and at Sam speculatively. 'We were already down here. Having a cup of coffee.' She indicated the still-warming percolator, shooting Gideon a look that said the-truth-is-usually-the-best-policy as she did so.

Sam knew damn well that the coffee percolator had been turned off when he went up to bed three hours ago; she had seen him check it.

'Merlin just seemed to go wild,' she added ruefully.

'Hmm. Well.' Sam gave a weary sigh. 'He seems to have calmed down again now,' he noted with some relief. Merlin was still lying beside the door, but no longer looking agitated. 'Back to bed, I guess.' He grimaced. 'Maybe we can all get another couple of hours' sleep before the next disturbance occurs,' he added ruefully.

Molly didn't need another disturbance to know she wasn't going to get any sleep tonight—thoughts of Gideon, of the intimacy they had shared, were enough to keep her awake for a week.

'How's Peter?' she prompted as the three of them went up the stairs.

Sam grinned. 'It seems a little trite to say "sleeping like a baby"—but that's exactly what he's doing. He's fine,' he assured her warmly. 'Although—' he sobered '—if Merlin carries on like that again I may just have to make him comfortable outside rather than in the house.' He didn't look at all happy at the idea.

'I'm sure it was just a one-off thing.' Gideon was the one to reassure him. 'Well, good night again, Molly.' He turned to her pointedly as they reached the top of the first staircase.

Her eyes widened at this obvious ploy to get rid of her. Gideon's guest bedroom was on the same floor as her own—surely it was more natural for the two of them both to say good night to Sam and go up together?

Not if you were regretting the intimacy that had occurred fifteen minutes ago. Then you would avoid being alone together again at all costs.

'Good night,' she said abruptly, not looking at either man before she hurried over to the second staircase and ran up to her bedroom, closing the door firmly behind her and leaning weakly back against it.

How could anyone be as changeable as Gideon obviously was? One minute telling her that she was beautiful, and how much he wanted her, the next coldly
wishing her good night?

He could if he didn't want anyone else to know that
the two of them had almost made love together. If he
regretted it had ever happened.

Well, she regretted it, too.

But not as much as she regretted the fact that she was
in love with him...

'I love Christmas, don't you?' Crys said happily the
next morning as they gathered in the sitting-room to
open presents beneath the tree.

'Gathered' as the result of Sam going along the hall-
ways knocking on all the bedroom doors to wake everyone up with the cry, 'Time to get up, Father Christmas
has been.'

And it was rather lovely. Sam had lit a fresh fire in
the hearth before waking everyone else, the lights
glowed on the tree, and even a little gentle seasonal
snow was falling as they looked out of the huge bay
windows.

'Love it,' Molly agreed with forced warmth.

One glance at Gideon had been enough—his expression was less than encouraging. Just normal Gideon,
really. It was the warm and sensual man of last night
who had been the exception.

'For you.' Sam handed her a gaily wrapped parcel,
standing in as Father Christmas as he distributed the
presents from beneath the tree.

One glance at the label showed that the lumpy-
looking parcel was from David. Molly glanced across
at him before opening it.

'Don't blame me,' he warned her laughingly as he strolled over to join them. 'I asked Crys, and she told me you collect them!'

In that case, Molly knew exactly what it was, and laughed as she opened the present and saw a cuddly pig holding a red rose in its trotter.

'Now I feel guilty that I only got you a book.' She grinned up at David.

'But what a book.' He grinned back. 'You probably won't get any sense out of me for the rest of Christmas. Okay, okay.' He laughed when Molly gave him a teasing look. 'You don't get much sense out of me anyway,' he accepted.

'Now, would I have said that?' she teased.

'Undoubtedly,' David said dryly.

Why was it so much easier to laugh and joke with David like this than it was with Gideon, the man she was in love with?

Probably because she *was* in love with him, she acknowledged ruefully.

And no longer had any idea what he felt for her.

Although, if the way he was scowling across the room at her now was anything to go by, after last night he held her in more contempt than ever.

'Another one for you.' Sam gave her a second package before resuming his present-giving duties.

Molly's hand began to tremble as she read 'To Molly, From Gideon' on the label. No frills or fancies about that. No 'love', either. Probably even 'best wishes' would have been asking for too much. And she would have preferred some cheerful robins on the wrapping paper rather than cold silver bells.

All of which meant she was totally unprepared for the beautiful cashmere scarf she found inside the package, so soft to the touch it felt like silk. But, more importantly, it was of the deepest pink—a colour Gideon had already assured her didn't suit her red hair.

'In contrast to the suit you were wearing on Sunday, this is the shade of pink that *does* go with your colouring.'

Molly looked up sharply as Gideon spoke, her hand closing convulsively on the scarf. She had been unaware until that moment that Gideon had crossed the room to stand beside her.

She swallowed hard. 'It's beautiful,' she told him sincerely. 'Thank you.'

He gave the ghost of a smile. 'Did it hurt to say that?'

She shrugged. 'Only a little.'

His smile widened. 'That's something, I suppose.'

It *was* something—considering she was slightly overwhelmed by his gift. 'Impersonal' was the way he had described the buying of her gift to him, and yet this scarf, obviously chosen to go with her particular colouring, couldn't be put in that category.

Crys stood up to announce briskly, 'Time for breakfast, I think.'

'I'll come and help,' Molly offered instantly, grateful for an excuse to stand up and break the air of intimacy that had been developing between herself and Gideon.

'We'll all help,' he said firmly. 'Just because both of you can, doesn't mean that you two women *should* do all the cooking around here.'

Which was probably about as close to a compliment for her cooking last night's meal as she was going to get from Gideon, Molly accepted ruefully.

'Oh, don't worry,' Crys paused to say laughingly. 'You aren't going to just sit here with nothing to do; you three men can amuse Peter for half an hour or so.'

And leave us two women alone to have a gossip in privacy, Molly guessed easily as she followed Crys to the kitchen. No doubt Sam had told Crys that Molly and Gideon had been downstairs together during the night, and her friend wanted to know all the details.

Something Molly had no intention of confiding in anyone—not even her best friend.

'So, come on—spill the beans,' Crys encouraged predictably as soon as the two women were safely ensconced in the kitchen.

Molly sighed, knowing that pretending not to know what her friend was talking about would be a waste of time; Crys could be dogged when she set her mind to it. 'I couldn't sleep and came downstairs for some coffee. Gideon had the same idea about half an hour later.' She shrugged dismissively.

Crys straightened from getting the eggs out of the fridge to eye Molly reprovingly. 'And that's it?' she said sceptically.

'More or less.' Molly nodded, determinedly turning her attention to laying the table.

How much more, Crys really didn't need to know.

Crys obviously wasn't of the same opinion. 'Well?' she prompted pointedly.

'Well, nothing,' Molly dismissed lightly. 'We both had a mug of coffee, and then Merlin started barking.' And in between that she had completely lost her heart, amongst other things.

'I don't understand the two of you.' Crys gave her an exasperated look. 'Gideon is gorgeous. You're beautiful—'

'Thank you,' Molly accepted teasingly.

'The two of you might at least have a flirtation—if

only to satisfy my romantic inclinations!' Crys complained frustratedly.

Molly couldn't help but laugh at her friend's disgruntled expression. 'Nice try, Crys.' She shook her head indulgently. 'But I've already told you—you're wasting your time where Gideon and I are concerned.'

'Obviously.' Crys frowned. 'But as two of my dearest friends, I do think you might have indulged me just a little.'

'Sorry,' Molly said unconcernedly.

'Oh, scramble these eggs,' Crys muttered frustratedly, before concentrating on preparing the other ingredients for breakfast.

Molly only wished she could distract her heart as easily as she seemed to have distracted Crys. But her heart wasn't as easily deceived. She knew without a doubt that she was in love with Gideon.

She flattered herself that she did quite a good job of hiding it as the day progressed. Not that it was too difficult to do, when Gideon seemed just as determined to avoid her company, too.

In fact, by the time they had all collapsed in the evening, after yet another sumptuous meal, Molly could honestly say that they hadn't exchanged more than a few words all day—and even those had only been of the polite category, such as 'Could you pass the salt, please?'

At least this respite from Gideon's company gave her a chance to rebuild her defences—defences that had been badly damaged during their closeness the night before. And she felt restored enough that she felt no qualms about joining Gideon and Sam for Merlin's evening stroll. In fact, after a day spent eating, chatting,

and watching the occasional programme on television—
a special Christmas *Bailey* being one of them—she wel-
comed the opportunity for some fresh air.

Although, from the scowl on Gideon's face as she
went outside, it seemed he would rather she hadn't
joined them.

Well, too bad. Sam was her brother, and this was her
Christmas, too.

The three of them walked in the grounds in silence
for some time, the moon's reflection on the light scat-
tering of snow on the ground making it a clear night.

'I'm glad you decided to join us, Molly.' Sam suddenly spoke heavily 'Gideon has told me exactly what's
been happening the last few days, and I think you
should know—'

'I disagree, Sam,' Gideon cut in harshly. 'In fact, I
don't think it's a good idea for you to talk about this,'
he added determinedly.

Sam turned to frown at the other man. 'Why not?'

'Because I don't.' Gideon's expression was harshly
forbidding, his face appearing all hard angles in the
moonlight.

Molly's own face, she knew, was pale; she had felt
the colour drain from her cheeks at Sam's opening comment. How could Gideon have told her brother what
had happened between the two of them during the
night? How *could* he?

'I disagree, Gideon,' Sam told the other man ruefully.
'I know you think you're being protective, but Molly is
far from being a child—'

'Obviously,' she snapped, utterly humiliated at the
thought of Gideon discussing her in those terms—with
her stepbrother, of all people. In fact, if he had been in

the least a gentleman he wouldn't have discussed last night with *anyone*.

'Molly—'

'Oh, forget it, Sam.' She interrupted his placating words impatiently. 'Gideon has spoken,' she snapped angrily, feeling the heated colour return to her cheeks as she turned to glare at Gideon in the semi-darkness. 'Too much, by the sound of it,' she accused furiously.

'Molly—'

'Stay out of this, Sam,' she told him coldly, her gaze still locked on Gideon. 'You are without doubt the most arrogant, self-opinionated, horrible man it has ever been my misfortune to meet,' she bit out accusingly.

'Molly, please let me explain—' Sam tried.

'Leave it, Sam,' Gideon rasped. His expression had become even grimmer at Molly's tirade of accusations, and his face was starkly etched against the moonlight. 'I'm sure Molly feels she is perfectly entitled to express her opinion of me.'

'Yes, but—'

'Too right I am!' she snapped, her hands clenched at her sides now. 'And arrogant doesn't even begin to cover what you are!'

He smiled without humour. 'Self-opinionated and horrible were two other descriptions, I believe,' he drawled hardly.

'Oh, I could go on,' she assured him scornfully. 'But, don't worry, I'm not about to,' she added scathingly as she saw how dismayed Sam was looking. 'I'm going back to the house now,' she told them both abruptly, before turning on her heel and marching furiously away.

The tears were falling hotly down her cheeks before

she had gone half a dozen steps, and she brushed them away impatiently as she began to run rather than walk.

How could he?

How could he?

CHAPTER TWELVE

'BUT you can't leave now,' Crys protested in dismay when Molly joined her in the kitchen before lunch the next day and told her of her intention of doing just that. 'It's still only Boxing Day,' she added incredulously.

Molly was well aware of what day it was. She was also aware, after yet another night of not sleeping, that she simply couldn't stay here a moment longer. If only so that she might go back to the flat she was renting in London and get some much-needed sleep.

Although that was far from the real reason for the decision she had come to during the wakeful night hours...

She would never forgive Gideon for confiding in Sam in the way that he had. Her humiliation had been complete the evening before, when Sam and Gideon had returned to the house and Gideon had ignored her. She'd sat talking to David. At least, she had been trying to talk to David—inside she'd been too disturbed to be able to think straight—before he'd made his excuses and disappeared upstairs to bed.

Molly had waited only minutes before doing the same thing, glad of the privacy of her bedroom to lick her wounds in private.

'I know what day it is, Crys,' Molly assured her friend lightly. 'But the traffic will be easier today for a long drive, and I still have lots of boxes to unpack.' She grimaced at the thought of the disorder she had left behind in her new flat in London.

145

Crys looked unconvinced by these arguments. 'But it's still Christmas.' She frowned.

'I've been here four days already, Crys,' she reasoned cajolingly. 'And it isn't as if you don't have other guests who will be staying on for several more days.' Her voice hardened at the thought that Gideon was one of those guests.

The real reason for her abrupt departure.

'I know that, but— Sam, talk some sense into Molly.' She turned to plead with her husband as he strolled in from walking Merlin. 'She says she's leaving today,' Crys told him frustratedly.

Molly could feel the blush in her cheeks as Sam paused in discarding his jacket to look at her with obvious surprise. But surely he more than anyone should realise that she simply couldn't stay on here another moment longer?

'Really?' her stepbrother murmured slowly.

'Really,' Crys echoed impatiently. 'Talk to her, Sam,' she encouraged forcefully.

Molly wasn't happy at breaking up everyone's Christmas like this, and was aware of how hard Crys had worked towards it, but at the same time she knew that the increasing tension between herself and Gideon was going to ruin it all anyway if something wasn't done to stop it. The only option appeared to be to remove one of the protagonists. And, as she doubted Gideon intended going anywhere, that only left her to be the one to make the move...

'Molly?' Sam prompted quietly.

'Sam, you know why I want to leave,' she told him exasperatedly.

'No,' he said slowly. 'I don't think I do. Crys, darling—' he turned to her smilingly '—would you mind if I just took Molly into my study with me for a while?'

'If you can persuade her into staying on you can keep her in there all day,' Crys assured him. 'In fact, if you can't persuade her, lock her in there until she agrees to stay.'

Sam chuckled ruefully, and even Molly had to smile at her friend's obvious frustration with her decision to leave today.

But there was nothing Sam could say to her that was going to make her change her mind...

'Is someone leaving?' Gideon questioned sharply as he walked into the kitchen.

Molly stiffened at the first sound of his voice, her expression guarded as she turned to look at him. 'I am,' she told him with determination.

Blue eyes looked at her calmly for several long seconds. 'Rather ungrateful of you, isn't it?' he finally murmured coolly. 'After all Sam and Crys have tried to do for us.'

She could feel the heat in her cheeks at this unmistakable reprimand. But he must know why she couldn't stay on here any longer.

'Don't give that another thought, Gideon,' Crys assured him. 'It's been a pleasure having you all here. It's just...' She grimaced. 'Sam is going to try to talk her into changing her mind,' she added confidently.

Molly wished they would all just let her leave and stop making such a fuss about it. After all, Sam at least knew exactly why she wanted to leave.

'Let me talk to her,' Gideon soothed.

That really was going too far.

'I don't think so, thanks,' she bit out disgustedly. He was the last person she wanted to talk to—the last person who could possibly persuade her into staying on here another day.

'Sam—' Gideon completely ignored her protest as he turned to the other man. '—I heard Peter stirring as I came down just now. And as Crys is busy preparing lunch... Come on, Molly.' He took a firm hold of her arm and practically marched her out of the room.

Molly tried to free herself. 'What do you think you're doing?'

'What do you think *you're* doing?' Gideon came back grimly, maintaining that grip of her arm. 'Stop fighting me, Molly; you'll only end up hurting yourself,' he advised coldly.

'As opposed to you hurting me?' she accused heatedly, not giving up on trying to pry his fingers from her arm. Not succeeding, either. But that didn't mean she wasn't going to keep trying.

Gideon came to an abrupt halt, turning her to face him in the hallway. 'Me?' he repeated harshly. 'What the hell have I done to hurt you?' he demanded impatiently.

Kissed her until her head spun. Made love to her. Made her fall in love with him.

She was breathing hard in her agitation. 'I have absolutely nothing to say to you—'

'Too bad—because I have a few things I want to say to you!' he ground out, pulling her into the sitting-room and finally releasing her as he closed the door firmly behind them.

The room where they had almost made love. The sofa where they had been so close. Too close.

Molly turned her back on the sofa, on those disturbing memories, glaring up at Gideon. 'Say away!' she challenged, her chin held defensively high.

Gideon looked down at her exasperatedly for several seconds, and then he gave an impatient shake of his head. 'You are, without doubt, the most stubborn person—'

'It takes one to know one.' Molly scorned.

'Doesn't it just?' he accepted ruefully, moving away to thrust his hands into his pockets. 'Molly, I don't think it's a good idea for you to leave here just now—'

'Surprise, surprise—I don't care what you think!' she told him incredulously.

His mouth twisted humourlessly. 'Do you think I don't already know that?'

Her eyes widened. 'Then why—?'

'Molly, there's something…' He paused, sighing exasperatedly at the situation. 'I really would rather not explain at this juncture.' He shook his head.

'Because there's nothing to explain,' Molly assured him scornfully. 'I already know you made a mistake kissing me the other night.'

'Is that what you think this is all about?' His eyes were narrowed to glittering blue slits, a nerve pulsing in his tightly clenched jaw.

'What else?' she said derisively. 'But you really don't have to worry about the other night, Gideon. I can assure you that I, for one, would much rather forget that it had ever happened at all!' She was breathing hard in her agitation.

'Do you think I don't know that?' Gideon drew in a sharp breath. 'You've made that all too damned obvious by the way you've been avoiding my company ever since,' he ground out accusingly.

'What did you want me to do?' Molly scorned. 'Fall all over you like some lovesick idiot?'

Again he gave that humourless smile. 'That would be asking too much.'

'Too right it would!' Her vehemence was all the deeper because that was exactly what she would rather have done.

It was what she wanted to do now...

Looking at him, being with him, brought home to her how much she loved this man, how much she wanted to throw herself into his arms and have him tell her that it was all right, that he was in love with her, too.

But she had stopped believing in fairy tales a long time ago, and was well aware that Gideon didn't love her. Oh, he might find her desirable—after the other night he really couldn't deny that—but it was against his own wishes to feel that way, was something he fought against all the time. And most of the time he succeeded...

'Okay.' He gave a heavy sigh. 'I accept that you want as little to do with me as possible. But do you have to leave to achieve that? I thought we had been managing to avoid each other quite well the last twenty-four hours?'

Oh, they had. She had. And so, from his comment just now, had Gideon. She just wasn't sure how much longer she could keep up this bravado, pretend not to give a damn.

But would she love Gideon any less for being alone in London? The answer to that was a definite no.

'I don't want to stay on here.' But even as she said it she knew her voice lacked the conviction it had had a few minutes ago.

'That isn't true, and you know it.' Gideon sighed. 'You don't want to stay here with me as a guest, too.

So the question is, do you want me to be the one to leave?'

Her eyes widened. 'Are you seriously offering?'

His mouth thinned. 'Yes, I'm seriously offering.'

Molly stared at him. Would he really do that? More to the point, could she ask him to do that?

Three days ago, when she had first learnt that he and David were to be guests here, too, over Christmas, she had considered Gideon to be an interloper, an intrusion on what should have been a family Christmas. But over those last three days she had come to realise that he wasn't an interloper at all, that he was as much a part of Crys and Sam's family as she was.

She moistened dry lips. 'I—' She broke off as she heard the doorbell ring. 'Are we expecting anyone today?' She frowned.

'I have no idea,' Gideon answered grimly. 'Wait here while I go and see,' he instructed abruptly, before striding from the room.

Wait here while I go and see, Molly's thoughts echoed resentfully; like hell she would.

Gideon had reached the door by the time she came out of the sitting-room, turning to give her a reproving glare as he heard her in the hallway behind him.

'It's okay, I'll get it.' He spoke to someone over Molly's shoulder.

Molly turned in time to see Crys shrug before returning to the kitchen.

Gideon was still glaring at her when she turned back. 'I thought I told you— Oh, never mind,' he snapped impatiently as Molly stood her ground, and reached out to wrench the front door open. 'Diana!' he greeted, his voice containing none of the ice of a few seconds before, when he had spoken to Molly.

'I hope I haven't arrived too early,' Diana apologised ruefully. 'Hi, Molly,' she said with a smile as she glanced around Gideon. 'Crys didn't actually specify a time when she invited me to come and spend the day with you all.'

'I'm sure you aren't too early.' Gideon opened the door wider for the doctor to enter. 'Especially as you seem to have arrived bearing gifts,' he added lightly, as the bag that Diana carried chinked tellingly.

'I couldn't possibly have accepted Crys's invitation without contributing in some way,' Diana Chisholm assured them, and laughed huskily. 'Besides, one of my partners has offered to be on call today—he has two aged aunts and his mother-in-law staying with him over the holidays,' she added pointedly. 'Which means I have an unexpected day off,' she said happily.

'That's good,' Molly told her sincerely, having a genuine liking for the pretty doctor. 'And I'm sure that if you do happen to have too much wine then Crys and Sam will be only too happy for you to stay here tonight,' she added.

'Oh, I doubt that I shall do that, but thanks,' Diana answered lightly. 'I noticed on my drive over here that there seem to be an awful lot of police cars in the area— no doubt on the lookout for drunk drivers going home from the pub.' She grimaced.

'Actually, you've arrived just in time to add your weight to the argument for Molly not to return to London today,' Gideon told the other woman lightly, and the gleam of challenge in his eyes was for Molly alone as he glanced across at her.

It was a glance Molly deliberately didn't meet as she turned to smile at Diana.

'Oh, no, you can't possibly,' Diana told Molly con-

cernedly. 'I moved here from London three years ago.'
She shook her head. 'It has to be the loneliest place on
earth at Christmas-time if you aren't with family.'

Any place was lonely if you weren't with people you
loved—the man you loved. Molly already knew that.
But being here with Gideon, when her love wasn't returned, was painful, too.

'Do stay, Molly,' Diana encouraged warmly. 'I did
so want to have a chat with you. I'm an avid fan of the
Bailey series, you know.'

Molly smiled. 'In that case it's David you should be
talking to, not me.'

Diana looked nonplussed. 'Oh, but he mentioned that
you're going to be in the new series with him?'

'Did he, indeed?' Molly laughed exasperatedly. 'David!'
She turned to open the library door—she had seen
David disappear in there an hour or so earlier. He was
still there, sitting in the window, gazing out at the snow-
covered landscape, a book lying untouched in his lap.
'And they say women gossip!' she teased as she preceded Diana and Gideon into the room.

David looked slightly surprised to see Diana, putting
the book down on the table to slowly stand up. 'What
did I do now?' He gave a quizzical smile, that smile
not quite reaching the sadness of his eyes.

'Never mind,' Molly dismissed lightly, moving to
link her arm with his, instinctively sensing that he had
spent enough time alone with obviously unhappy
thoughts. 'As there's no sun today, I have no idea
whether or not it's over the yard-arm yet—but let's all
go and join Crys and Sam in the kitchen and open up
a bottle of wine while we help prepare lunch.'

'Sounds like a good idea to me.' David nodded.
'Lead on, MacDuff,' he invited lightly.

Somewhere between opening the red wine Diana had brought with her, pouring it into glasses, and helping Crys prepare the vegetables for lunch, Molly's decision to leave was forgotten by all of them.

Deliberately so by the others, Molly was sure. But with Diana's arrival it seemed churlish to pursue her plans to leave. Besides, Crys had prepared her delicious trout dish for lunch—a culinary experience that no one should miss.

'It was a pity you didn't get back the other evening to join us in going to church.' Gideon spoke lightly to Diana as the six of them sat around the dining-table, eating their main course.

Diana, sitting to his left, grimaced slightly. 'I don't know what it is, but babies always decide they want to be born on Christmas Day. This one also decided it couldn't wait for the ambulance to arrive and take its mother to hospital, and I ended up delivering it myself, just after midnight. A healthy little boy, I'm glad to say, and mother and baby nicely tucked up in bed shortly after one o'clock. A home birth has to be the most wonderful experience,' she added softly.

Molly gave Gideon a sharp glance, sure that he had deliberately mentioned Christmas Eve in an effort to see whether or not it had been Diana's car in the driveway that night. From what the doctor had just told them, it obviously hadn't.

But if that had been Gideon's intention Molly could see he certainly wasn't going to share that knowledge with her—unless she was very much mistaken, once again he was deliberately avoiding meeting her gaze.

In fact, he had been noticeably aloof towards her during the whole meal as she'd sat across the table from him, while at the same time warmly considerate to Diana Chisholm.

Encouraged by Crys, she had to acknowledge. Her friend, having taken Molly's uninterest in Gideon literally, now appeared to be deliberately encouraging a friendship between Gideon and Diana.

Jealousy wasn't an emotion that Molly had known for a long time, and never as she felt it now—aware of every word spoken between Gideon and Diana, every laugh they shared.

'What are you up to now?' she demanded of Crys as she followed her friend into the kitchen to help carry in the desserts.

'Sorry?' Crys looked at her blankly.

Deliberately so, Molly was sure, when she saw the mischievous twinkle in her friend's laughing grey eyes. 'Don't play the innocent with me.' She grimaced wryly. 'Gideon and Diana?' she said pointedly as Crys continued to look at her blandly.

'Oh, that.' Crys nodded slowly.

'Yes—that!' Molly snapped tersely.

'Aren't you being a little dog in the manger, Molly?' Crys came back knowingly.

Molly could feel the blush in her cheeks at her friend's correct assessment of the situation. 'Don't be ridiculous, Crys,' she bit out shortly.

Crys gave a husky laugh. 'Is that what I'm being?' She raised blond brows as she moved briskly about the kitchen, preparing the whisky cream to go with oranges that had been marinading in liquor overnight.

Molly sighed heavily. 'You know that you are. Gideon is— Crys, you simply can't be this blind—you must know it's you Gideon loves!' she burst out forcefully.

Crys came to an abrupt halt, giving Molly a stunned stare. 'Now who's being ridiculous?' she finally said incredulously. 'Of course Gideon isn't in love with me.' She shook her head. 'He's James's brother,' she added dismissively.

'So?' Molly returned exasperatedly. She couldn't believe her friend was unaware of how Gideon felt about her.

'So he's James's brother!' Crys repeated impatiently, her smile rueful. 'Really, Molly, I don't know how you came to such a conclusion, but I can assure you—'

'Gideon himself,' Molly cut in frustratedly.

'What?' Crys gasped incredulously.

'From watching Gideon whenever he's with you,' Molly said tersely. 'He adores you, Crys—'

'I hope that he does,' Crys cut in. 'Because I adore him, too. After James died, and then my parents six months later, Gideon was the only family I had left. But that's all it is, Molly,' she added frowningly. 'All it's ever been.'

She shook her head with certainty. 'Not on Gideon's side.'

'Yes, on Gideon's side,' Crys insisted evenly. 'Molly, is this the reason you've been staying clear of Gideon? Because if it is—'

'I've been ''staying clear of Gideon'', as you put it, because he doesn't like me,' she came back impatiently.

'Rubbish!' Crys came back, just as firmly. 'If you want my opinion, Molly, then you haven't given him a chance to like or dislike—'

'I don't,' she cut in firmly.

'Okay.' Crys shrugged. 'In that case, carry the oranges and cream through for me while I bring the *crème brûlées*.' She gave an exasperated shake of her head. 'I really don't know what you were thinking of, Molly,' she added reprovingly as she picked up the tray. 'Gideon is the big brother I never had.'

But just because that was the way Crys felt about the relationship, it still didn't mean that Gideon felt the same way...

'Move, Molly,' Crys ordered determinedly. 'And if I'm wrong, and you do want Gideon, then I advise you to start showing it a little more,' she advised. 'Otherwise Diana may just pip you to the post,' she added wryly.

If she wanted Gideon...

She wanted Gideon more than she had ever wanted anything or anyone in her life before. But—

There was always a 'but' in her dealings with Gideon.

And Molly still thought Crys was wrong in her dismissal of Gideon's feelings towards her...

CHAPTER THIRTEEN

'YOU never did answer my question earlier.'

Molly tensed at the sound of Gideon's voice, turning slowly to find that he had joined her where she sat on the hearthrug in the sitting-room, playing with baby Peter's toes while the other adults all sat in chairs—or lay on the sofa in Crys and Sam's case—dozing after the filling lunch they had all eaten. Until this moment she had thought Gideon asleep in a chair, too.

'You like babies, don't you?' Gideon murmured huskily before she had a chance to answer his initial statement, gently touching Peter's hand as he sat on the rug beside them.

She frowned, keeping her voice low so that they shouldn't disturb the others with their conversation. 'Doesn't everyone?'

He shrugged. 'I haven't always found that to be the case, no,' he answered ruefully. 'For instance, my own mother wasn't particularly maternal.' He grimaced.

Molly's eyes widened. 'But she had you and James.'

He nodded. 'I was the necessary "heir". James's arrival, ten years later, as the "spare", was an accident she never let anyone forget. Including James himself,' he added grimly. 'She walked out on all of us, taking most of my father's money with her, I might add— when James was only four. I was fourteen.'

Molly blinked, surprised by this confidence coming from a man she knew to be completely sufficient unto

158

himself. But maybe this was an insight into the reason he was like that…?

Gideon gave a humourless smile as he glanced up and saw the expression on her face. 'Not exactly what you expected, was it?'

What *had* she expected? From his obvious wealth and self-confidence now, yes, she had assumed that Gideon had always led a charmed life—as had James seemed to. But these revelations seemed to point towards a completely different sort of childhood from the one she had imagined for them.

But why should Gideon assume she had expected anything? That she had even given his past life a second thought…?

'My father did the best he could, of course. He sent me to university, engaged nannies and then found a boarding-school for James,' Gideon continued softly. 'But unfortunately he died from a heart attack when I was twenty and James only ten.'

Not the background she had imagined at all for this often seemingly arrogant man!

She frowned slightly. 'Why are you telling me these things, Gideon?' she asked slowly, voicing her puzzlement.

He gave a husky laugh. 'Truthfully? I have no idea!' he admitted self-derisively. 'Perhaps it was watching your gentleness with Peter just now. Or to explain why a family Christmas like this is special to me.' He gave a rueful shake of his head. 'Or, more probably, I just drank too much wine with lunch!'

Molly stared at him for several seconds—at the way his hair fell endearingly over his forehead, the softness in his eyes; even his mouth was not set in that forbidding line as he gazed down at Peter.

'Which question were you referring to a few minutes ago?' she prompted huskily.

Gideon glanced up at her. 'About my being the one to leave here. Because if you want me to go—'

'I don't,' she hastily assured him; it would be cruelly insensitive of her to even suggest he leave this place where he obviously felt so much at home, when he had no other family to go to.

That could have been the reason he had told her those things about his childhood, of course—although somehow she very much doubted that Gideon was a man who would ever play upon another person's feelings in that way; he was simply too emotionally aloof to ever welcome an emotion in others that might be interpreted as pity.

He seemed to guess some of her thoughts, his mouth twisting scornfully. 'Don't feel sorry for me, Molly,' he rasped harshly. 'I can assure you I'm actually doing very nicely, thank you!'

Yes, he was. He was obviously financially secure, and had a career that made him much in demand. It was only in the area of having a family of his own that Gideon seemed lacking, but Molly felt sure that had to be from personal preference; she didn't doubt for a moment that there were dozens of women who were attracted to his blond, arrogant good looks, who would willingly have married him and shared their life with him.

Herself, to name but one…

She straightened, knowing she must never let him guess that. 'And I can assure you I don't feel in the least sorry for you, Gideon,' she told him briskly, keeping her face averted as she bent down to pick Peter up, at once feeling more relaxed as she held his scented softness against her. 'He's adorable, isn't he?' she murmured indulgently as the baby nuzzled into her neck and promptly fell asleep.

Gideon gave a brief smile. 'He's certainly found a comfortable place to sleep!'

Molly gave him a searching glance, frowning slightly. Had there been a slight edge of wistfulness in Gideon's tone, or had she just imagined it?

You just imagined it, she told herself firmly, knowing from the way he had virtually ignored her during lunch that there was absolutely no reason why Gideon should ever want to fall asleep on her shoulder.

If it was her shoulder he had been referring to...

Her gaze narrowed on him questioningly, and was instantly answered by Gideon's mocking grin.

No, it wasn't her shoulder he'd been referring to.

'Let me take him from you and put him in his cradle,' Gideon offered, reaching out to take the baby, his fingers brushing lightly against Molly's breast as he did so.

Molly's skin seemed to burn where those fingers had lightly touched.

Had that touch been accidental or deliberate? she wondered as she watched Gideon cross the room and carefully place the baby in the cradle before covering him with a blanket. She still had found no answer to that question when Gideon returned to stand beside her.

'Shall we leave them to sleep and take Merlin for a walk?' he suggested huskily, even as he held out a hand as an offer to help pull her to her feet.

Molly looked at that long, artistic hand, clearly remembering its touch upon her skin, its caresses seeking, finding her complete response. It would be dangerous to her own peace of mind to go outside alone with him. But not to go would be just as unacceptable to her heart!

'That sounds like a good idea,' she agreed abruptly, ignoring his hand to get agilely to her feet unaided.

Gideon gave a rueful smile in acknowledgement of her obvious rejection, his arm falling back to his side. He thrust his hand into his denims pocket. 'Wrap up warm,' he advised briskly as they walked down the hallway to the kitchen. 'There's more snow forecast for later this afternoon.'

Molly felt slightly self-conscious as she wrapped the deep pink cashmere scarf he had given her for Christmas around the bottom half of her face and neck before pulling on her thick sheepskin jacket. It was such a beautiful scarf, and so soft to the touch, that it would be churlish not to wear it just because Gideon had given it to her.

'Here—let me,' he offered as the scarf became slightly dislodged by her coat collar. His fingers were warm against her cheeks as he deftly pulled the scarf back into place. 'It really does look wonderful against the rich auburn of your hair,' he stepped back to remark admiringly. 'But, then, I knew that it would.' He nodded his satisfaction.

Molly looked up at him from beneath her lashes, slightly breathless at the compliment. 'Thank you,' she accepted self-consciously.

Gideon chuckled at her obvious wariness. 'You're welcome. Come on—let's go.' He threw open the door, a blast of icy cold air instantly hitting them.

It really was cold outside, and Molly was grateful to be able to burrow down in her scarf, her hands thrust into the deep pockets of her coat. The scarf about her lower face also served to hide the blush to her cheeks caused by Gideon's unexpected compliment.

'You didn't think I would remember you, did you?' Gideon remarked quietly after they had walked in silence for several minutes. Merlin was happily running on ahead, obviously fascinated by the cold white stuff that covered the ground.

Molly gave Gideon a sharp glance. 'Sorry?'

'From James and Crys's apartment over three years ago,' he answered evenly.

So they were back to that, were they? So much for hoping they might be learning a new tolerance between them.

She turned away, hunched down in her jacket. 'I don't recall ever giving it a second thought,' she answered dismissively.

She didn't remember giving it a *second* thought because she had followed that by dozens of others once she'd known Gideon was to be at Peter's christening.

She gave an impatient sigh. 'Gideon, did you invite me to share this walk with you just so that you could pick another argument with me?'

His face lit up in a smile, eyes laughingly blue. 'Strangely enough, no!'

Molly gave an irritated shake of her head. 'Then you have a very funny way of showing it!'

'Funny, strange—not funny, ha-ha?' he drawled derisively.

'Oh, definitely funny, strange!' she answered impatiently, stopping abruptly as they reached the gate that would take them out into the country lane. 'Gideon, how many times do I have to tell you that I did not—however briefly—ever have an affair with James?'

He met her gaze unblinkingly, his expression unreadable. 'I don't believe you ever have told me that…'

Molly's frown deepened. 'But—of course I have!' she dismissed before walking on, stiff with indignation, only to find herself swung back to face Gideon as he took a firm hold of her arm. 'Let me go, Gideon,' she instructed coldly.

To her surprise he instantly did exactly that, holding up his hands before stepping away from her. 'No, you never did, Molly,' he assured her softly.

She blinked, thinking back over the conversations they had had together over the last four days—most of them unpleasant. And that unpleasantness had merged into one long battle of wills between the two of them. When they hadn't been in each other's arms, of course.

No, she couldn't remember specifically telling him that she hadn't had an affair with James. But even so…

'Well, I did not have an affair with your brother! Or, more to the point, Crys's husband,' she added, indignation starting to rise in her voice. 'Crys is my best friend,' she added firmly. 'She always has been. Always will be. And I would never, ever do anything that might hurt her. I think having an affair with her husband might just have done that, don't you?' she scorned.

'Undoubtedly,' Gideon acknowledged quietly.

'Well, she won't be hurt, because I didn't.' Molly was warming to her subject now, wanting to get all of this off her chest while she had the chance to do so. 'Yes, I was at Crys and James's apartment that night when Crys was away, but not because I was having an affair with James. And if you knew anything about me at all—'

'I believe you.'

'—you would believe me when I tell you that's—'

'I believe you.'

'—the truth... I beg your pardon?' She looked at Gideon warily as his words finally penetrated her indignation.

Gideon drew in a deep breath, looking down at her intently. 'I said, I believe you, Molly,' he repeated softly.

She blinked, wondering if this wasn't another ploy on his part, if he wouldn't later somehow twist her words to suit his less-than-flattering opinion of her.

'Oh,' she said noncommittally.

Gideon gave a heavy sigh. 'Now it's you who doesn't believe *me*.'

'Can you blame me?' Her eyes flashed darkly. 'You've done nothing but accuse me of one indiscretion or another since we met again on Sunday. To accept that you now believe my version of what happened over three years ago is a little hard to take.'

He grimaced. 'I'm sure it must be,' he acknowledged. 'Although, if you think back carefully over the early part of this conversation, you might recall that you didn't actually give me your version of what happened. I told you—I believe you, anyway,' he pointed out huskily.

Molly, after days of this man's taunts and put-downs, was beginning to feel slightly as if her legs were being taken out from under her. Where was Gideon's antagonism now? Why was he being so nice to her?

'Would it help if I were to apologise for all the less-than-flattering remarks I've made to you over the last few days?' Gideon asked grimly.

'It might,' she allowed warily.

It was a wariness Gideon seemed all too aware of, and he sighed heavily. 'Molly, I think the two of us need to talk, and I'm not sure here is the best place.'

'Everything all right here, sir?'

Molly turned sharply at the sound of that voice, her eyes widening as she saw a policeman standing on the other side of the gate. She had been so taken up with this unexpected exchange with Gideon that she hadn't even noticed the police car parked beside the road, let alone this man's approach.

Gideon gave the policeman a reassuring smile. 'Everything is fine, officer.' He nodded. 'Miss Barton and I are just taking the dog for an after-lunch stroll.'

The other man nodded, eyeing the watchful Merlin with a certain amount of caution. 'You'll be two of the guests staying at Falcon House, sir, with Mr and Mrs Wyngard?'

'Yes, we are.' Gideon moved slightly in order to take a proprietorial hold of Molly's arm. 'Is there any news?'

The policeman nodded. 'I'm just on my way to see Mr Wyngard now.'

'With good news, I hope?' Gideon prompted guardedly, his fingers tightening slightly on Molly's arm.

The policeman looked grim. 'Depends on how you look at it, sir,' the policeman answered noncommittally. 'Well, I'll just pop along and see Mr Wyngard now, and leave the two of you to continue your walk,' he added briskly. 'Nice day for it,' he added, before strolling off to get into the squad car, giving them a wave as he drove off towards Falcon House.

Molly frowned as she watched him drive away, totally lost as to what the conversation between the two men had been about. She had no idea what news, good or bad, the policeman could possibly have to give to Sam.

But obviously, from their brief conversation, Gideon knew.

CHAPTER FOURTEEN

'OKAY.' Molly turned determinedly towards Gideon. 'Exactly what is going on? And please don't insult my intelligence by answering ''nothing'',' she added forcefully.

Gideon gave the ghost of a smile. 'I wasn't about to do that,' he drawled. 'But I think it might be better if we return to the house and I leave it to Sam to explain,' he added grimly.

'But—'

'It really isn't up to me, Molly,' Gideon cut in firmly. 'But maybe once he's explained you'll excuse some of my behaviour over the last couple of days,' he added frowningly.

'I wouldn't count on it!' Molly told him hardly, even as she turned and began to walk back to the house.

'That's what I'm afraid of.' Gideon caught up with her after only a couple of strides, Merlin trailing along obediently behind him.

Molly gave a disbelieving snort. 'You aren't afraid of anything!'

'Oh, but you're wrong there, Molly,' he answered softly, causing her to give him a sharp look. 'I'm very much afraid you aren't going to forgive me once Sam has made his explanations,' he told her grimly.

She gave an exasperated shake of her head. 'I'm sure any lack of forgiveness on my part isn't going to keep you awake at night!'

His expression became even grimmer. 'You'd be surprised!'

'Yes—I would,' she dismissed scornfully.

Gideon drew in a controlling breath. 'I've really messed things up between us, haven't I?'

'There's never been any "us" to mess up,' Molly assured him.

His hands were painful on her arms as he pulled her to a stop before they entered the house. He turned her to face him, his expression harshly remote. 'Will you at least agree to talk to me in private after the policeman has said his bit and gone?'

'What would be the point?' She sighed.

'Will you?' He shook her slightly.

'If that's what you want—yes!' she agreed, impatient to be inside.

'It is what I want.' He nodded grimly.

'Fine,' Molly dismissed. 'Now can we go inside?'

He gave an impatient snort before releasing her, following behind as she hurried into the house.

No one was asleep when Molly entered the sitting-room a few seconds later. Crys and Sam were sitting on the edge of the sofa now, and David and Diana were all attention, too, as they sat forward in their chairs. The policeman held all their attention as he stood in front of the fireplace, nodding acknowledgement of Molly and Gideon's arrival in the room even as he continued with what he had been saying.

'Unfortunately Miss Gibson was involved in an accident about two miles from here just over an hour ago,' he informed them briskly. 'She's dead, I'm afraid,' he added evenly.

Miss Gibson? Rachel Gibson? Sam's ex-fiancée of twelve years ago? The woman who had told all those lies about Sam to the newspapers after he'd broken their engagement because he had realised she was emotionally unstable? The woman who had made all of their lives such a misery twelve years ago—so much so for Sam that he had moved to the wilds of Yorkshire in order to escape her vitriol?

'Oh, no...' Crys had gasped at the policeman's news. 'I hated what she was doing to us, but... How awful!' She turned her face into Sam's chest.

Sam's arm closed protectively about his wife. 'How did it happen?' he asked the policeman quietly, his face ashen.

'Her car went off the mountain road and down into a deep ravine,' the other man informed him. 'She was already dead when the rescue services arrived,' he added apologetically. 'I'm sorry to bring you such bad news over Christmas, sir,' he added regretfully. 'Although, in view of the charges against her, if we had caught up with her...!' He trailed off pointedly.

'Yes,' Sam acknowledged heavily.

'What charges?' Molly turned to Gideon with wide, bewildered eyes. 'Is that *Rachel* Gibson they're talking about?' she demanded disbelievingly.

'It is,' Gideon answered hardly. 'Come on,' he encouraged, his arm about her shoulders as he guided her out of the room. 'You don't need to hear any more of that,' he told her briskly, and he took her into the library, sitting her down in one of the armchairs before moving to pour her some whisky from the decanter on the table. 'Please drink some of it,' he said, as he came down on his haunches beside her to give her the glass.

Molly didn't need any prompting, totally numb from the shocking news she had just heard.

But though her emotions felt numb, her brain seemed

able to coolly and calmly dissect the events of the last few days, to pick out all the incidents that at the time hadn't seemed to make any sense.

She looked at Gideon with clouded brown eyes. 'She's been stalking Sam, hasn't she?' she guessed heavily. 'She was the one making those telephone calls on Christmas Eve. And that night,' she continued determinedly, 'the noises outside that so disturbed Merlin… Even his getting shut in the shed in that way,' she recalled dazedly. 'It was all her, wasn't it?'

'We believe so,' Gideon said grimly. 'Although we'll never really know now, I'm afraid,' he added heavily.

Molly gave a shiver at the reason why they would never know.

Twelve years ago Rachel had been a blight on all their lives, her lies encouraging the press to hound Sam, and the whole family, until their parents had been forced to move out of their home. Molly had had to begin anew in another school, and Sam had isolated himself in the wilds of Yorkshire.

But, even so, Molly knew that none of them would have wished the other woman dead…

'It was her,' Molly said with certainty. 'But how did she…? The newspaper article about Peter's christening!' she realised with a groan.

'Sam seems to think so,' Gideon confirmed gently.

'But—it—I—it's been twelve years!' she gasped. 'Twelve years, for goodness' sake!'

'Yes,' Gideon acknowledged heavily. 'But something happened over the weekend—something that seems to have sent her completely over the edge.' He frowned grimly. 'The police have been looking for her ever since.'

Those charges the policeman had mentioned…

'What?' Molly breathed intently. 'What happened over the weekend?'

'Molly, she's dead.'

'What happened?' she demanded through gritted teeth.

Gideon drew in a deeply controlling breath. 'She killed someone. The man she was living with,' he continued firmly at Molly's shocked gasp. 'She discovered him with another woman and—she killed him.' He frowned darkly.

Molly swallowed hard. 'How?'

'Molly, you don't need to know—'

'Tell me,' she demanded harshly.

'She stabbed him,' he said flatly. 'The woman he was with managed to escape, but unfortunately the man had died from his wounds before the police got there.'

Molly felt sick, waves of nausea washing over her as she realised that it could have been Sam—that if he hadn't broken their engagement twelve years ago Rachel could have…

'Bend down and put your head between your knees,' Gideon encouraged gently, taking the glass from her hand as she did exactly that.

It took several minutes for the waves of nausea to stop, the light-headedness to dissipate. But they were minutes when her brain once again seemed capable of functioning without any help from her.

She straightened. 'You knew about all of this,' she said accusingly. 'All this time you've known—'

'I've known for precisely one day,' Gideon corrected her firmly. 'Since I mentioned my misgivings to Sam after you went to bed that night and he came clean on the subject. One of those telephone calls he had to return on Monday morning was to the police,' he explained, as Molly would once again have spoken accusingly. 'Rachel Gibson had been reported as being seen in the area, and, following investigations, they discovered that she and Sam had once been engaged...' He shrugged. 'The police wanted to inform Sam of the—incident, only as a matter of courtesy, because of their past connection. I don't believe they really thought she would come after him here.'

'Then they were wrong, weren't they?' Molly rasped. 'Finally knowing where Sam was, seeing that photograph, seeing his happiness with Crys and Peter. My God, did Crys know about all this, too?' She frowned as the thought suddenly occurred to her. She'd have a deeper respect for Crys if she *had* known; to all intents and purposes, apart from that scare with Peter, Crys had seemed caught up in the gaiety of Christmas.

Gideon smiled without humour. 'Sam doesn't have any secrets from Crys.'

'Unlike you with regard to me,' Molly snapped, picking up the whisky glass and downing the contents. 'I suppose now you're going to accuse me of being a lush again?' she challenged, two fiery spots of angry colour in her cheeks.

It wasn't logical, and she knew that it wasn't, but nonetheless she couldn't help her feelings of anger towards Gideon for treating her as if she were a child who couldn't handle the truth. She felt the same anger towards Sam, too. But Gideon was the one here in front of her, and as such he was the one who would bear the brunt of her anger.

'Molly—'

'Don't touch me!' she told him fiercely, brushing past him to stand up.

Gideon eyed her warily and slowly stood up. 'Molly, there was no point in worrying you, too—'

'Don't tell me whether or not I should worry!' she snapped furiously, her eyes glittering brightly. 'I'll worry if I want to—not when someone else decided that I should!' she continued illogically. 'God, you're an arrogant—'

'I advise you to stop right there,' he warned coldly.

'—pig,' she concluded challengingly. 'A chauvinist pig to boot,' she continued wildly. '*You* were the one who stopped Sam from telling me the truth.' She realised what had happened now, what it was Sam had wanted to talk to her about. But he had been stopped from doing so by Gideon's warnings of caution. 'I can hear it all now. "Don't tell the little woman",' she mimicked. '"It will only worry her".'

'It wasn't like that—'

'Yes, it was,' she snapped hardly. 'It was exactly like that! Well, do you know something, Gideon Webber? You can go to hell,' she continued, without giving him an opportunity to answer.

She turned sharply on her heel and ran from the room, taking the stairs two at a time until she reached the sanctuary of her bedroom, where she threw herself down on the bed, her anger quickly turning to tears.

She cried for poor, sick Rachel, and the obsession for Sam that had never completely left her. She cried for the mess that was Gideon and her, for all the misunderstandings between them. But most of all she cried because in spite of everything she knew she still loved him.

'Hey,' Crys chided gently as she moved to sit beside Molly on the bed a few minutes later. Molly had been crying so deeply she hadn't heard her friend enter the room. 'Molly,' she said firmly, 'it's over now. Come on.' She pulled Molly into her arms, hugging her tightly as the tears finally began to stop. 'Who are you crying for, Molly? Poor Rachel? Or Gideon?' she added astutely.

Molly moved back to look at her friend. 'Is it so obvious that I'm in love with him?'

Crys gave her an encouraging smile. 'Only to me. Gideon doesn't have a clue, I can assure you,' she added ruefully. 'In fact, from what he said to me just now, he seems utterly convinced that you hate him.' She looked questioningly at Molly.

She swallowed hard, wiping the tears from her cheeks. 'It's him who hates me,' she contradicted. 'And all because—because... Crys, there's something I should have told you long ago,' she said huskily. 'Something about James. And...and me.'

Crys frowned. 'Yes?'

Molly closed her eyes briefly, taking a deep breath before she began talking, knowing it all had to come out now, and that Crys should have been told long ago. 'Do you remember my disastrous love affair with Derek? Of course you do.' She answered her own question with obvious self-derision. 'You tried to warn me at the time about the dangers of falling in love with a man so recently separated from his wife—that very often they patched up their differences and were reconciled. I didn't listen, as you know.' She sighed heavily. 'And I ended up getting very hurt when Derek did exactly that.'

Crys looked confused. 'You don't still love him, do you?'

'No, of course not,' Molly dismissed instantly. 'I'm not sure I ever did,' she added huskily. The way she now felt about Gideon made that other love pale into insignificance. 'Maybe I was just flattered.' She sighed again. 'He was an internationally known actor, very good-looking, and it was *me* he wanted to be with! At least I thought it was at the time...' She shook her head. 'I was devastated when he returned to his wife.'

'I know that.' Crys nodded, still looking puzzled.

'Yes,' Molly said firmly. 'But what you don't know—what I've never told you—is that the night Derek went back to his wife I got very drunk—'

'You were entitled,' Crys replied. 'He wasn't exactly gentle about it, if I remember—just arrived at a party with her one night. A party where he was supposed to be meeting you,' she recalled disapprovingly.

Molly winced at the memory. 'The night I got dr—'

'Alcoholically challenged,' Crys corrected decisively. 'You drank a little more than you would usually, that's all. James assured me that you certainly were not drunk.'

Molly blinked, her mouth feeling very dry. 'James did...?'

'Of course,' her friend dismissed. 'I was glad that you went to him. Sorry I wasn't there to help, of course, but James assured me he had done a good job of taking care of you.'

'He did,' Molly confirmed numbly. 'But—I—you *knew* about that night?'

'Well, of course I did,' Crys assured her lightly.

She frowned dazedly. 'But I... All this time...' she shook her head '...and you've never said.'

Crys gave a rueful smile. 'What could I have said? Derek was a very selfish man, and he hurt you very badly; there was no point in my bringing up the subject again when you obviously didn't want to talk about him.'

'But the night I stayed at your apartment—'

'What of it?' Crys asked. 'Look, Molly, you're my best friend and I trust you implicitly, just as I trusted James, so what was there for me to say about that night? Without reminding you of Derek's duplicity, that is,' she added grimly.

Molly shook her head dazedly. 'I can't believe you've known all this time that I stayed at your apartment with James when you were away...'

Crys smiled. 'I've known and never for a moment thought there was anything wrong with it. Why should I have done?' she said unconcernedly.

'Well, Gideon certainly thought there was something wrong with it!' Molly snapped disgustedly.

'Gideon did?' Crys looked more puzzled than ever, and then her brow cleared in understanding. 'Oh, you mean because he called in to see James that morning and saw you there? Molly, Gideon didn't think that you and James were having an affair, did he?' She gasped as the idea suddenly occurred to her. 'No! He can't have done. Can he?' She frowned dazedly. 'He did, didn't he?' she realized incredulously. And then she began to laugh.

'Crys, it really isn't funny,' Molly told her disgruntledly. She was relieved that Crys had known the truth all along, but utterly bemused by her friend's reaction to knowing what conclusion Gideon had come to concerning Molly's presence in Crys and James's apartment that morning.

'No, it really isn't,' Crys agreed, sobering slightly. 'You and Gideon are incredible, do you know that?' She stood up. 'You think he's in love with me—which he most definitely is not,' she added firmly as Molly would have spoken. 'And Gideon thinks you had an affair with James—which you most definitely did not. You know, for two very intelligent people, you've both been incredibly stupid.'

'Thanks!' Molly grimaced, not sure she agreed with Crys's summing up of the situation at all.

'You're welcome,' Crys assured her dryly. 'Not completely stupid, of course,' she continued conversationally. 'Somewhere amongst all this confusion the two of you have managed to fall in love with each other anyway, so I suppose I can forgive you.'

'Gideon isn't in love with me,' she cut in dismissively.

'Oh, yes—he is,' Crys said with certainty. 'Who do you think sent me up here because you were so upset? Who do you think is even now pacing up and down my kitchen wearing out the flagstones as he waits for me to go back downstairs and reassure him that you're okay?'

Molly swallowed hard, suddenly still, a slight hope beginning to burn somewhere deep inside her. 'Gideon…?' she said hopefully.

'The one and only.' Crys nodded, pulling her to her feet. 'Come downstairs with me—'

'I can't!' Molly resisted, jerkily shaking her head. 'I really can't, Crys,' she added, as her friend gave her a look of reproof. 'What if you're wrong?'

'I'm not,' Crys assured her.

'But if you are?'

'I'm not,' her friend repeated firmly. 'Although maybe the kitchen isn't quite the place for…' She paused, obviously thinking. 'Okay.' She nodded as she came to a decision. 'You stay here and I'll send Gideon up—'

'He won't come,' Molly told her with certainty.

'We'll see,' Crys murmured speculatively. 'Just don't stay up here together all afternoon—otherwise, knowing Sam, he's likely to come looking for the two of you and demand that Gideon make an honest woman of you!' She grinned.

Molly frowned. 'I wish you would stop making a joke out of all this, Crys.'

'Can I be chief bridesmaid?' Crys asked conversationally. 'I've never been a bridesmaid, you know, and—'

'Oh, go away!' Molly told her irritably.

'I'm going,' her friend assured her. 'But no attempting to climb down the drainpipe after I've gone,' she warned on her way out of the room. 'You won't look a very elegant bride with your leg in plaster!' She grinned again as she made her parting shot.

Molly gave an exasperated shake of her head once she was alone, thinking that Crys was turning into as much of a tease as Sam.

Although that didn't change the fact that even now Crys was probably down in the kitchen talking to Gideon.

Was Crys right? Would Gideon come up here to see her once he had spoken to Crys?

She would have the answer to that question in the next few minutes.

CHAPTER FIFTEEN

'CRYS said that you're feeling a little better...?'

Molly's heart leapt as she turned to see Gideon standing hesitantly in the bedroom doorway, his face guarded, the expression in his deep blue eyes wary.

She swallowed hard before speaking. 'Er—yes, I'm feeling better.' She nodded. 'I—I'm sorry I shouted at you. Before.'

Wonderful, Molly, she inwardly chided herself; she sounded like a tongue-tied idiot.

But that was probably because she *felt* like a tongue-tied idiot!

Just because Gideon was here, as Crys had said he would be, that did not mean anything more than that he wanted to apologize for upsetting her concerning not telling her earlier about Rachel Gibson.

'Perfectly understandable in the circumstances,' he allowed abruptly. 'It was arrogant of me to ask Sam not to tell you.'

Arrogant, yes—but it could also have another interpretation... 'Why did you do it, Gideon?' she prompted.

He drew in a harsh breath. 'I—do you think I could come in?' He grimaced. 'It's a little—public, standing out here in the hallway.'

Considering that besides themselves only David had a bedroom on this floor of the house, and he was probably still in conversation with the others downstairs, she wouldn't exactly have called it 'public'. But if Gideon wanted to come into her bedroom...

'Please do,' she invited, standing awkwardly in front of the window as he entered the room and closed the door quietly behind him, her hands twisting tightly together as she eyed him warily.

Gideon gave a strained smile obviously as uncomfortable as she was.

'I—' Molly hesitated, shaking her head, not really sure where to begin. Or what she was actually beginning!

Gideon drew in a harsh breath. 'Will it help the—the situation if I tell you that I'm not in love with Crys?' he bit out abruptly. 'That I never have been.'

Molly felt a sinking sensation in her stomach. Okay, so he wasn't in love with Crys, but that didn't mean he was in love with her.

She bit her lip painfully to stop it trembling. 'I was never in love with James, either,' she told him huskily. 'And I certainly didn't have an affair with him,' she added firmly.

'I know that.'

She nodded. 'Crys will have told you—'

'No,' Gideon cut in determinedly. 'Crys didn't tell me anything.'

Her eyes widened. 'But—'

'She didn't have to,' he continued evenly. 'Molly, I know that I owe you an apology for—for the things I've said to you over the last few days.' He gave a self-disgusted shake of his head, thrusting his hands into his pockets. 'I saw you in James's apartment that morning and I—'

'Drew your own conclusions?' she finished heavily.

Gideon shook his head. 'No, that isn't what happened at all.' He gave another strained smile. 'I looked at you that morning, your hair all tousled, your face sleepy, your long legs bare beneath that ridiculous shirt, and I—' He drew in a harsh breath. 'You were the most beautiful woman I had ever seen!' he told her gruffly.

Molly's eyes widened incredulously. 'I looked awful! My hair was a mess, my face all puffy, and James's shirt was the only thing I could find to pull on when I needed to go to the bathroom. You can't possibly have... Did you really think me beautiful?' She looked at him dazedly.

'Really.' Gideon nodded self-derisively. 'But it appeared you belonged to my brother,' he added hardly.

'But I didn't,' Molly told him exasperatedly. 'I never did. How many times do I have to tell you that?'

'You don't,' he assured her heavily. 'You see, it made no difference; I fell in love with you anyway that morning—'

'You couldn't have done!' Molly gasped disbelievingly.

'Oh, yes, I could.' Gideon nodded. 'And I spent the next few months telling myself what a fool I was—that just being attracted to you was dangerous, that falling in love with you was an act of madness, that it would be better for everyone if I just forgot I had ever seen you. I almost succeeded in believing that, too.' His mouth twisted ruefully. 'Until I saw you again the morning of the christening...'

'You were so horrible to me,' Molly reminded him breathlessly, that faint glow of hope she had known when talking to Crys now starting to explode inside her.

Had Gideon really just told her that he had fallen in love with her more than three years ago?

'I know,' he accepted flatly. 'Deliberately so. I simply couldn't believe that I still felt the same way about you, that those years might just as well not have been.

Your relationship with James, what the knowledge of it might do to Crys—' He gave a self-disgusted shake of his head. 'In spite of all that I was still in love with you.'

Molly gave a pained frown. 'But you said just now that you believed me when I said I didn't have an affair with James…?'

'No.' He sighed. 'What I actually said was that I *know* you didn't have an affair with him. And I know that because over the last few days I've come to know you, Molly. You're not only the most beautiful woman I've ever seen, you are also the kindest, most compassionate woman I've ever known. Your loyalty to Crys and Sam is unmistakable, your love for them, too. Your compassion for David is only to be admired. And as for your gentle caring for Peter… Molly, you would never have allowed yourself to have an affair with James even if you had been in love with him!'

'No,' she acknowledged. 'But I wasn't in love with him. I did think myself in love with someone else, though,' she hurried on, as Gideon would have spoken. 'A man separated from his wife. The night before you saw me at the apartment he had gone back to her,' she confided evenly. 'Not my finest hour.' She grimaced.

'But don't you see, Molly? It doesn't matter,' Gideon said forcefully. 'Unless you're still in love with him, of course,' he added uncertainly.

Uncertain? Gideon? It certainly wasn't a feeling that Molly would normally have equated with him!

But hadn't he just told her that he had fallen in love with her at first sight? That he'd only had to see her again over three years later to know that he still loved her?

She moistened dry lips. 'No, I'm not still in love with

him, Gideon,' she told him quietly. 'How could I be when I'm in love with you?' she added almost shyly.

His eyed widened, emotion blazing in those dark blue depths. He took a step towards her, then stopped, hesitating.

Molly was the one to take the two last steps that took her into his arms; in fact she almost threw herself into them, her arms about his waist as she held him tightly to her. 'I love you, Gideon,' she told him forcefully. 'I love you so much.'

His hands moved up to cup either side of her face. 'Will you marry me?' he asked emotionally. 'Will you? I swear I'll love you until the day I die!' He looked down at her intently. 'Molly, I only wanted to protect you by not telling you about Rachel Gibson. I've never thought of you as less than you are, and I never will,' he promised. 'I just want to protect and love you for the rest of our lives!'

'Yes,' Molly accepted chokingly, wanting to laugh and cry at the same time. 'Oh, yes, Gideon, I'll marry you!'

As he moved to kiss her with infinite gentleness, with all of the love he felt for her in that loving caress, Molly knew that she had at last found the man she truly loved, and who truly loved her.

'You look adorable,' Gideon assured her lovingly. 'Although I'm not sure it was a good idea for me to suggest you put on one of David's shirts.' He frowned darkly. 'It just makes me want to throw you on the bed and make love to you!'

Molly laughed huskily. 'Not here, darling.' She looked around pointedly at the crowded studio, at the director and technicians all on the *Bailey* set, and David already in the bed, waiting for her to supposedly appear out of an adjoining bathroom.

'Later, then,' he promised gruffly.

'Later,' Molly echoed throatily.

The two of them had been married for three months now. Crys had got her wish to be chief bridesmaid, with Sam acting as Gideon's best man.

It had been three months of pure happiness as far as Molly and Gideon were concerned. The two of them were working together a lot of the time, too, as Gideon had turned out to be the new designer of all the sets for the *Bailey* series. Neatly answering Molly's question of how an actor, David, and an interior designer, Gideon, could possibly have met before they had all spent Christmas together.

But it was because of Gideon's involvement with the new *Bailey* series that he had been able to have some input into the nude scene that had been mentioned over Christmas. Knowing of Molly's aversion to it—and having certain objections of his own concerning his wife appearing nude on public television—he had come up with the suggestion of Molly undressing off-set and coming back wearing David's shirt.

The fact that he had made the suggestion at all, so reminiscent of the first time they had met, told Molly how unimportant all that had been. If she had needed any reassuring. Which, after three ecstatic months as Gideon's wife, she most certainly didn't.

'Actually—' she leaned into Gideon '—I think it's as well that I do this scene now. Another couple of months and I won't be able to.'

Gideon looked down at her concernedly. 'Why not? Molly, what's wrong?' His arms moved about her protectively.

'Absolutely nothing.' She laughed reassuringly. 'But it's going to be interesting seeing Sam cope with introducing a pregnant girlfriend for Bailey,' she added teasingly, gazing lovingly into her husband's face as the importance of what she had just said slowly dawned on him.

'Molly…?' he finally gasped, his arms tightening about her as he stared down at her disbelievingly.

Molly snuggled into the warmth of his chest. 'In about seven months' time Peter is going to have a little cousin,' she confirmed huskily. Her happiness was overwhelming at the knowledge that she carried their child.

'I—you—how…?' Gideon was obviously having trouble speaking at all, but his eyes glowed brightly with love as he looked down at her.

'You know very well *how*,' Molly teased him huskily. 'And, yes, it was you and I.' She nodded happily. 'Isn't it wonderful?'

'Wonderful,' he confirmed, slightly dazedly. 'Oh, Molly, I do love you,' he told her intensely.

'And I love you,' she assured him seriously. 'All my life,' she promised.

'All my life,' Gideon echoed forcefully, before his mouth claimed hers in a kiss of infinite sweetness.

'I hate to interrupt,' David called out dryly several minutes later, 'but I'm in danger of genuinely falling asleep if you don't soon make your entrance, Molly.'

Gideon raised his head to grin down at her ruefully. 'I think your presence is required, my love.'

'I think David is just a little full of himself after his weekend away; apparently he drove up to Yorkshire at the weekend and took Diana Chisholm out to dinner,' she told her husband speculatively.

'That's good news.' Gideon smiled.

'Isn't it?' She grinned up at him. 'Maybe we're going to have another wedding in the "family" soon.'

Gideon's smile turned to an indulgent chuckle. 'You're getting as bad as Crys with your matchmaking.'

Molly reached up to gently touch his cheek. 'Maybe because, like Crys, I want everyone else to be as happy as we are,' she told him seriously.

Gideon shook his head. 'They couldn't possibly be,' he said with certainty.

No, she didn't think they could. She had never known such happiness, such contentment, as she had found being Gideon's wife.

'Molly!' David called out complainingly.

'I have to go.' She grimaced ruefully.

Gideon nodded. 'We'll celebrate our good news later.'

'We could go to Crystal's,' she agreed happily; Crys's restaurant was one of the most exclusive in London, but Gerry, the manager, always managed to find a table for 'family'.

Gideon's smile became intimate. 'I wasn't thinking of going out.'

'Even better,' Molly agreed instantly, feeling a glow deep inside her at the promise in Gideon's gaze.

'Molly, if you don't get in here in the next ten seconds I'm going to come and get you.' David warned.

'Later,' Molly told Gideon as she hurriedly turned to leave.

'Always,' he called after her.

What a wonderful, lovely word!

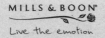

MILLS & BOON®

Live the emotion

1204/01b

Modern
romance™

THE BILLIONAIRE BOSS'S BRIDE by Cathy Williams

On her first day as PA to Curtis Diaz, Tessa makes a bad impression on her sexy boss. It sparks a turbulent business relationship – and underneath passion is surging! Curtis wants to know why he desires Tessa like no other woman – and offers a proposition she can't refuse…

HIS PREGNANCY BARGAIN by Kim Lawrence

Megan knows that seeing sexy Lucas Patrick is wrong, but how else can she foil her mother's matchmaking? He pretends to be infatuated with her…then he decides to make his acting role real, and Megan finds herself in a bigger fix: she's pregnant!

THE BRUNELLESCI BABY by Daphne Clair

Ruthless Italian tycoon Zandro Brunellesci has decided his dead brother's child must be taken away from Lia - his brother's mistress would be an unsuitable mother. Yet she seems to have changed and Zandro even finds himself attracted to her…

THE ITALIAN'S MISTRESS by Melanie Milburne

When it comes to Anna Stockton, Lucio Ventressi wants only one thing – vengeance for the way she dumped him. Anna needs money and Lucio makes her an offer: he'll pay her to be his mistress for three months. Anna has no choice but to agree…

Don't miss out…

On sale 7th January 2005

Available at most branches of WHSmith, Tesco, ASDA, Martins, Borders, Eason, Sainsbury's and all good paperback bookshops.

MILLS & BOON

Stroke
of **Midnight**

Three gorgeous
men...one sexy
New Year Party!

Jamie Denton   Carrie Alexander   Nancy Warren

On sale 7th January 2005

*Available at most branches of WHSmith, Tesco, ASDA, Martins,
Borders, Eason, Sainsbury's and all good paperback bookshops.*

**Volume 7
on sale from
2nd January
2005**

Lynne
Graham

International Playboys

*Crime of
Passion*

FREE!

4 Books
and a surprise gift!

We would like to take this opportunity to thank you for reading this Mills & Boon® book by offering you the chance to take FOUR more specially selected titles from the Modern Romance™ series absolutely FREE! We're also making this offer to introduce you to the benefits of the Reader Service™—

- ★ **FREE home delivery**
- ★ **FREE gifts and competitions**
- ★ **FREE monthly Newsletter**
- ★ **Exclusive Reader Service offers**
- ★ **Books available before they're in the shops**

Accepting these FREE books and gift places you under no obligation to buy, you may cancel at any time, even after receiving your free shipment. Simply complete your details below and return the entire page to the address below. You don't even need a stamp!

YES! Please send me 4 free Modern Romance books and a surprise gift. I understand that unless you hear from me, I will receive 6 superb new titles every month for just £2.69 each, postage and packing free. I am under no obligation to purchase any books and may cancel my subscription at any time. The free books and gift will be mine to keep in any case.

P4ZEF

Ms/Mrs/Miss/Mr ....Initials ....
BLOCK CAPITALS PLEASE
Surname ....
Address ....

....
....Postcode ....

Send this whole page to:
UK: FREEPOST CN81, Croydon, CR9 3WZ